Books also by William E. Lemanski

Lost in the Shadow of Fame - The Neglected Story of Kermit Roosevelt; A Gallant and Tragic American

Adventures in Distant and Remote Places

Murder
IN
TUXEDO PARK

WILLIAM E. LEMANSKI

SUNBURY
P R E S S
Mechanicsburg, PA USA

Continue the Enlightenment!

introduction

This story is a fictional account of Tuxedo Park in the latter 19th Century. The characters portrayed are also fictional. However, the setting of Tuxedo Park is an authentic and historic gated community which was home to many of the very wealthy and influential titans of that period. The author has attempted to capture the ambiance of that locale and the lifestyle and character of its inhabitants during that gilded period.

Besides being the home of the very wealthy, the listing of the Park's residents during the last one and a quarter century has included famous names in politics, science and the arts. Beginning in the early years, the Tuxedo Club's membership included J. P. Morgan and Cornelius Vanderbilt. The records of the Park's, Saint Mary's Church list in 1896, when 14-year-old Franklin Delano Roosevelt

Modern-day photo of Tuxedo Park, stone entrance gate by architect, Bruce Price, late 19th Century

1

served as godfather for the baptismal of his cousin, Sara Roosevelt Collier, a resident of the Park. Franklin Roosevelt's mother, Sara Delano Roosevelt signed as the godmother in the parish register. During two Memorial Day services in the 1920's, Superintendent of the United States Military Academy at West Point, General Douglas McArthur, was guest speaker.

Other notables who have lived in the Park in later years include: former United States Congresswoman, Katharine St. George; actors, Richard Kiley, Robert Duvall, Whoopie Goldberg and Fred Gwynne.

Also resident were New York State Governor, Thomas E. Dewey and Alfred Lee Loomis, who was a polymath American attorney, investment banker, philanthropist and scientist. Loomis was one of the early developers of radar in his Tuxedo Park, mansion laboratory.

William E. Lemanski
Tuxedo Park, New York
October 1, 2015

one

Despite the languor that the passing years hold on my memory, I wish to say, nay, I feel compelled to express before I pass, to both relive and record the following events, as best I can, of those dark, dastardly and evil days in Tuxedo Park, many years ago. Now in my 69th year, I must divulge to the public the evil that stalked this community. The events, which are unknown to this day, and I fear, even when exposed, will be un-believed.

John Thomas
December 24, 1951

The long, narrow, serpentine road curved beneath the overhanging trees in dappled shadows as it wound through the quiet forest. Barely noticeable in the shadows, a large, stately mansion, will occasionally emerge, setback a distance from the road and shielded by a stone wall or iron gate or a barrier of yew. Some with sprawling gardens, others with boathouses fronting the lake and still others with courtyards and horse stables.

The imposing structures were the abodes of the rich and influential titans of Wall Street and the sporting class of the early 20th Century. The gated enclave of Tuxedo Park, nestled in the Ramapo Hills, a mere thirty miles north of Manhattan, was one of the first planned communities in the country as well as one of the most affluent. And why not, after all, the new elegant dinner jacket worn by the upper class and heads of state is named after Tuxedo. This new look in fashion occurred when the New York gossip columnists would swoon over the Hamptons in the summer along with the Autumn Ball and winter sports of Tuxedo Park as the seasons revolved. The Park was even the national epicenter of that ancient, arcane and elitist sport called court tennis, not to mention the home of some of the nation's finest thoroughbred racehorses.

Originally created as a forested playground by tobacco magnate, Pierre Lorillard, the uniqueness of the Park became just as eccentric as some of its inhabitants. Aside from its thousands of acres of stonewalled seclusion, it boasted miles of electric street lighting and its own electric generating plant while over ninety-nine percent of the country still burned gas lamps. Just outside its imposing stone entry on the Post Road, a small community, actually a company town was established to house the hundreds of European laborers imported by Lorillard to build his many miles of roads and stone fencing and who also served as the maids, butlers and general staff of the Park's inhabitants.

One of which, I became.

* * *

Perhaps one of its most eccentric and brilliant property owners was James I. Montague-Smith, who was referred to as Monti. His middle name was bestowed in honor of the famous British engineer, Isambard Kingdom Brunel, the brilliant and equally eccentric 19th Century character who built the Great Western Railway and the first propeller-driven transatlantic steamship. Monti's father was a British expatriate who, besides working with Brunel in the early years, became a colleague of Nicola Tesla, Edison and many other of the shining stars of 19th Century electrical science. Although also an engineer, Monti's father focused more on the economic growth of the technology and became fabulously wealthy accruing a fortune from his many business interests.

Monti, although holding degrees in medicine and engineering, lived as a country squire and relied on his vast inheritance while spending his time dabbling in various experiments in his Tuxedo Park laboratory. Curiosity was his driving force having never found a diversion that wouldn't interest him. His twelve-hour days were spent sequestered in his lab pursuing arcane investigations into obscure and sometimes bizarre topics. Science fiction was not his forte, but rather he questioned "by what force would a pencil drop to the floor?" And why would mass exert attraction to other mass, and just what defined the nature of one's spirit, and so on into many of the inexplicable and esoteric phenomena of nature's mysteries.

His main interest was the human mind, questioning by what derangement or character flaw a person would create heinous crimes while others rose to genius. He was amazed when considering that the human body consisted of many billions of cells, each its own little factory processing and producing energy while being in synchronism with its counterparts. And most curiously, all communicating with the brain. This strange jelly-like organ functioning as the master control center. He was well aware of the recent advances in electrical science and surmised the linkage between the brain and the body's extremities may be through electrical impulses. His obsessive personality focused on the minutia of his enquires, even forcing him to acquire human brains surreptitiously from a shady local undertaker. Despite possessing the ghoulish artifacts, arrayed in jars in his lab, he was unable to chemically unlock their secrets.

His outward appearance seemed as bizarre as his interests. While working in his laboratory he would wear a lab coat, or smoking jacket, slippers over bare feet and he would don a red Egyptian tarboosh. When travelling he would be attired in a tweed jacket and short trousers, knee socks and wear a pith helmet while puffing on the ever-present lamplighter pipe. He would occasionally carry, rather than a cane or walking stick, an African knobkerrie, a relic from his days living with the Zulus in South Africa. His quirky habits even baffled his butler and all around personal assistant, Jones, whom he treated as a military batman and all around gofer.

I first met Doctor Montigue-Smith when, as a young boy, he hired me to clean-up around his sprawling gardens.
J.T.

At the other end of the social spectrum of Tuxedo Park was the Colonel Henry Stafford McKinnon. Unlike the young Monti, Stafford was an overweight and cranky anachronism whose birth preceded the Mexican War. He made his money in railroading following the War Between the States when the government was bestowing massive parcels of real estate to private interests for developing the Great Plains and beyond. He gained his rank in that great conflict along with a wooden leg, having lost that appendage to a rebel cannon ball at Gettysburg. Some said his aggressive, cantankerous nature originated from the loss of that leg and the ongoing sensation that it still existed.

Among the other two hundred or so families, was the young socialite, Emily Post, daughter of the well-known architect, Bruce Price. Price designed many of the Park's mansions and a number of commercial buildings in the community outside the gate, including the town library and train station. Even the famous author, Mark Twain spent time in the Park.

Generally, the Park inhabitants enjoyed and guarded their isolated seclusion. Many kept townhouses in the city while spending their weekends and extended summer vacations in the Park. The railroad built a station in town and ran a special, exclusively private bar car on the 6:15 run from Grand Central Station to accommodate the carousing and card games of the wealthy passengers. Indeed, the Tuxedo Park swells loved their opulent lifestyle and splendid, bucolic seclusion.

However, my gruesome story would be dishonestly lacking without introducing Quincy Mortimer Thompson, known as Quint by his friends.
J.T.

The son of one of the Park's founding members, Quincy Mortimer Thompson was a rich, lazy playboy whose only qualities were his skills at the elite equestrian sport of polo, and, wooing the young ladies. In fact, as a member of the Oyster Bay Polo Club at Oyster Bay, New York, Quincy organized a tournament between the polo club and the Hurlington Club, the renowned home of the English polo set. Thereafter, this famous event was continuously held, even following the Great War while Quincy was a frequent competitor in the early years.

two

Although only 8 a.m., as usual, Monti would partake of his morning cocktail bitters and pastry. As Jones climbed the winding stone stairway up to the tower laboratory, he stumbled over the house cat and dropped the tray sending it clanking down the three flights of stairs with the cat following in a fit of screeching terror. After replenishing the tray, he deftly ascended the stairs again and knocked on the heavy oak door.

"Sir, your morning constitutional has arrived."

From the inner sanctum of the lab a strained voice yelled, "Jones, you clumsy oaf! Enter."

As Jones opened the door, he spied Monti balancing against a wall, upside-down performing a handstand. Concealing his face was his smoking jacket all akimbo across the floor. Jones deftly placed the tray down asking, "And what may we be doing Sir?"

"I'm attempting to analyze the effects of gravity on the digestive tract. And what was that racket? I almost lost my balance!"

"Sinbad was lounging in an awkward position on the stairs, Sir"

"Well perhaps you and Sinbad should also analyze the effects of gravity and damn that retched cat!"

"Shall I prepare your tie and tails for the ball, Sir, it is this evening?" Just then a flushed Monti performed a lopsided back flip regaining his footing right side up.

"Oh, it is this evening, isn't it. Well I guess I should attend, despite it being the largest congregation of dullards and nitwits in the county."

* * *

Beginning in the 1880s, Park residents held a yearly autumn ball at the Tuxedo Club—a coming out party for New York's debutantes in the stately building opposite Tuxedo Lake. Within little more than a decade, this gaudy venue would become the origin of the evil and deadly intrigue that enveloped the Park and its inhabitants.

The club's huge circular ballroom contained a stage where on that fateful night an orchestra continuously played Strauss waltzes along with popular tunes of the day as the splendidly attired couples whirled across the floor in merriment. Others congregated at the bar discussing the latest row over the drop in the silver market and how the latest panic may affect them. Quincy was seen to be wearing his scarlet red, cut-down dinner jacket which became the namesake of the Park. Unnoticed was the absence of the most vivacious young women in the Park, Sara Mills, who incidentally was the apple of Quincy's eye.

The eighteen year old Sara was the daughter of Jacob Mills, one of the leading importers of rubber in the country. His interests ranged from Southeast Asia to the Amazon Basin. He was also a doting and protective father to the beautiful Sara. Normally, Sara would be accompanied to the affair by both her father and mother until the formal ceremony later in the evening announcing her introduction to society. However, as the evening progressed, all three remained absent. After an hour or two of the festivities, Sara's parents rushed into the ballroom in a state of extreme agitation and cornered the orchestra leader. At once the music stopped and the dancers focused on the stage in startled silence.

"Our daughter is missing!" A near hysterical Mills shouted. "She is nowhere to be found! We looked everywhere!" On learning this, an audible gasp was heard throughout the crowded hall. The orchestra leader immediately suggested a search party be formed. Quincy, simply disbelieved what was being said insisting that she just got temporarily waylaid, probably visiting a friend. The cranky Colonel McKinnon suggested calling the town constable.

Monti, who arrived as the Mills blurted out their frantic statement, immediately took charge and began questioning Jacob and his wife. "When was she last seen and by whom? What was she wearing and what was her demeanor?" Nothing the parents said shed any light on her mysterious disappearance. She was last seen at around six in the evening as her ever doting mother lovingly assisted in adjusting her corset and helping her don her evening gown. Then Sara apparently retired to the study to retrieve a book before attending the ball. The parents then lost track of her as they prepared for the ball themselves.

Monti, immediately began selecting and advising men from the crowd to breakup and scour areas of the Park: their homes, top to bottom including their stables and any who kept conservatories, the church, and the village hall, and to reassemble in the club at 2 a.m. To expedite searching the eight miles or so of roads, he sent a messenger into town informing the constable and requesting the fire brigade to be called out for the roadway search.

He then accompanied the Mills to their home to conduct a search of his own. He first began in her bedroom looking through Sara's books, letters and any notes of correspondence he could find. Pictures of any of her acquaintances were scrutinized, particularly those of any males. He even rummaged through her clothing wardrobe, leaving nothing in the room unanalyzed. Nothing of evidentiary value surfaced. He then went into the study, a large room with a vaulted ceiling. He meticulously picked over the long rows of bookcases spanning each wall for anything that looked unnatural or any position within the thousands of books left open indicating a removed book. He then looked over the floor, desks and lounge chairs and he even analyzed the lamps and underneath the chairs and sofas. As he approached the double French doors leading to the rear of the mansion, he noticed one of the double door handles was turned up ninety degrees indicating when the door was opened, it was not returned down when the door was closed. He surmised a hasty exit was taken from the mansion.

After finding and lighting an oil lamp, he proceeded through the double doors to the stone terrace beyond. Down on all fours, he picked over the cobblestones in a pattern and then continued down the slate walkway to the lake, finding nothing but the multicolored autumn leaves drifting down in the cool breeze. However, when approaching the bank, he spied two sets of footprints in the loose soil and what appeared to be skid marks, the type which would be created while dragging a boat to and from shore. The footprints were one of a large boot size and the other indicated the type of imprint a small, high button shoe would make, but in a somewhat smeared fashion.

Jones arrived at the lake just as Monti was down on his knees scrutinizing the markings and asked his well-worn question: "And what may we be doing Sir?" Monti gently tapped the earth with his knobkerrie commenting in a low, distressed voice, "Jones, I fear we are dealing with a malevolent case of skullduggery! Jones, fetch my plaster and a pot of water. I must take impressions."

As 2 a.m. approached, the men began filing back to the club along with the arrival of the town constable. Each reported finding nothing as Monti informed the constable of Sara's mysterious disappearance and his findings at the lake edge. Constable Charlie Dillon was an old time cop beginning his career with the Pinkerton Agency out west where he chased train robbers and various other desperadoes. Now he was simply an overweight, over-the-hill fixture in town with a propensity for overindulgence with a too frequent bottle of distilled corn. From past experience, he learned to avoid any serious discussion with the great Montague-Smith on any topic besides the weather. But even that mundane a topic could draw Monti into a string of polysyllabic nouns and adjectives that totally befuddled the poor simple cop.

After listening to everyone's disheartening report, Monti began his detailed dissertation on the footprints: "Upon inspecting the Mills' home interior and finding not a thing, I noticed the library external doors in an awkward, inconsistent and careless position, indicating a hasty entry or exit by someone. This finding encouraged me to pursue what may be of interest out-of-doors. There I chanced upon two sets of footprints by the lakeshore that were very interesting in their configuration; one was that of a large size, indicating a man wearing boots. The boot's sole style indicated the possibility of it being a riding boot as it was somewhat narrow and pointed, that which is suitable for easy entry into a stirrup. The depth to which it sunk into the soil spoke of it belonging to a very heavy man. The other footprints were clearly belonging to a woman of light weight wearing the type of high button shoes currently in style. A very interesting feature of her prints were the elongated pattern which indicates to me that she walked somewhat unsteady, as if being helped or pushed along. The really telling mark displayed the drag pattern of a boat being released into the lake. I fear we are confronted here with an abduction. So therefore, I suggest you all congregate at sunrise, and begin walking the periphery of the lake inspecting the bank and I, along with the constable will simultaneously visit all of the boathouses and interview their owners."

Constable Dillon spoke up effecting a haughty and official tone suggesting the lake shore should be inspected immediately while not considering the early morning mist that always formed on the lake in this season. In a condescending manner, Monti replied, "And just how effective do you think that inspection would be in the dark? And how much detail would be missed, or evidence trampled?" That abruptly ended the discussion.

* * *

Groups of men began circling the miles of lake shore in the early hours as the constable and Monti began visiting the private boathouses and dock owners. Most of these property owners were already privy to the emergency while in attendance the night before, and those who weren't certainly heard about it by now. Based upon Monti's fastidious attention to detail, stretched the process of questioning the owners and investigating their individual properties, long into the afternoon. Word was relayed around the lake that the foot teams hadn't turned up any clues along the lake, nor had Sara returned—the mystery continued.

Dillon rapped the heavy bronze knocker against the oak door of the Colonel McKinnon mansion. Wearing a robe and slippers, the colonel answered the door himself, having released his butler earlier in the morning. After a brief spate of questions, the two sleuths, with the colonel in tow, walked down the long dock to the boathouse. Upon entering the clapboard building, the three were stunned with the sight before them. Sprawled across the walkway that extended between a small sloop and a rowboat, was the body of Sara Mills. Even in death she was resplendent in evening gown and sparkling jewelry. A cursory touch of her flesh indicated she was cold with rigor mortis having already stiffened her limbs. Dillon stood back as Monti slowly paced back and forth working himself into a quiet frenzy of curiosity. Not the concern with encountering the corpse of a young, formerly vivacious woman—and a neighbor to boot—or the driving desire to bring a cruel and dangerous killer to justice, but the thrill and challenge of a major puzzle.

He began methodically inspecting her from her shoes, working up along the flowing silk gown. Inspecting every square inch of the fabric, her fingernails, the jewelry on her wrist and around her neck and even scrutinizing her earrings for any clues. After analyzing her face and hair, there were no obvious signs of struggle or trauma, in fact, had it not been for her cold, white, waxy appearance she simply appeared to have laid down for a rest, lying face up, eyes open with her head tilted back.

As Monti investigated the head and neck area of the corpse, he seemed to momentarily detect a faint odor of chloroform. This was a very mild and fleeting sensation. He also spotted a thin crust of blood within her right nostril. Using a pair of tweezers, he gently expanded the nose flesh noting the dried blood appeared to continue up into the region of her sinus.

A thorough investigation of the two boats, the walkway and the interior of the boathouse rendered no clues as to the cause of death or who may have accompanied her. Dillon mindlessly theorized that she wandered here for a secret tryst on her own and may have suffered a cardiac distress scaring away her lover. The colonel appeared shaken and flabbergasted that she was found on his property commenting that "with her great beauty she must have had many admirers." Monti reserved judgment, as he could not reconcile the strange, momentary odor of chloroform and the blood, although a burst vessel could have rendered the discharge. His instinct was to perform an autopsy before reaching any conclusion.

Monti then began questioning the servants. As both the colonel and his wife attended the affair the night before and arrived prior to the time of Sara's disappearance, both clearly were not suspects in any possible foul play. However, the manor staff remained within the house all evening, this coupled with the grisly discovery in the boathouse placed them all in suspicion if a crime did occur.

One by one they all were ruled out. None had seen Sara or heard anything in the boathouse during the night and all were able to corroborate each other's movements during the night. All except the butler who supposedly spent long hours isolated in the cellar alone, inventorying the numerous bottles of wine and other spirits in the wine cellar. Hence, his early morning departure from the house after working late. At the moment, the whereabouts of the butler were unknown, and this would require a follow-up.

Both the town and Tuxedo Park were very rural in the latter 19th Century. The only law enforcement within the region was Constable Dillon. The nearest practicing physician, with a medical school background (besides Monti) was twenty miles away in the county seat of Goshen. Travel was arduous and time-consuming. Therefore, Monti's immediate reaction was to transport the body to his laboratory and perform an autopsy himself. The longer the corpse remained in situ, the greater the deterioration and a reduced opportunity to determine the cause of death.

When hearing this the constable vehemently objected and attempted to assert his authority, "She clearly died of natural causes, and besides, consider the scandal to the family and the Park if it was discovered that she was not chaste! And this even before her coming out ceremony! I cannot condone this."

Monti, always oblivious to human sensibilities and social niceties in favor of science, and determining fact, arrogantly waved off the constable's concerns. "So you will ignore reality and the possibility of a murderer roaming about for the purposes of etiquette?" "I simply don't agree with your farfetched theory" the constable responded. Monti had no recourse but to defer to the constable's authority. They didn't even question the absent butler.

The local undertaker, who, as the elected coroner in town, declared Sara's death a tragic natural occurrence. The Park's gossips concluded she probably planned a brief rendezvous with a secret lover and tragically fell ill, scaring away her paramour. The entire population attended Sara's sad funeral at St. Mary's and she was laid to rest in the church graveyard. Within a short period Park life returned to normal.

The end of the 19th Century was an exciting and turbulent time in America. The Wild West was no more, ushering in numerous new business interests expedited by completion of the transcontinental railroad. The telephone was already invented as electric usage was spreading and the country was clamoring for retribution following the sinking of the Maine in Havana Harbor, all of these events and many more created a very restless period, indeed. But the changing times seemed to have little effect on the Park.
J.T.

Most of the business titans in Tuxedo Park had managed to weather the continual boom and bust periods quite well; the panics seemed to have little effect on their prosperity. Monti was approaching early middle age and felt a sense of nervous urgency as he began pursuing his esoteric interests with increased vigor.

The Park's inhabitants settled down to their regular lifestyle of socializing at the club, golf course, and endless rounds of cocktail parties. Very little was discussed regarding the death of poor Sara who has resided in the cold ground these past eighteen months. However some peculiar and tragic events had been occurring. Little Tommy Baxter's body was discovered floating, face down in the lake near the dam last winter. The general belief was that the tragic event occurred when he ventured on the ice and fell through. The gaping gash on the back of his head was thought to have happened when he hit the hard concrete of the dam. Jim Walker, the Park's popular syce and horse expert was found trampled to death in one of the stables. Although these events saddened the Park, they were simply accepted as natural tragedies. The latter 19th Century was a rough and tumble time to live with many dangerous possibilities lurking close at hand in everyday life. The only questioning cynic regarding these events was Monti, who was considered brilliant, but also an extreme eccentric, not to be taken seriously on most issues. While greatly respected for his superior intellect, his fellow Park neighbors simply could not accept his strange ways.

The ending of the great Columbian Exposition was Monti's last important scientific involvement in the public arena and he was now beginning an odyssey into the mysteries of the mind. He started by spending a considerable amount of time across the Hudson River at the Sing Sing penitentiary at Ossining. The institution was built in 1826 and housed some of the most notorious criminals in the country. The prison became well publicized in 1891 when its new electric chair, which became known as "Old Sparky," was used for July 7th, the mass execution of four condemned men.

Monti's interest, however, did not focus on the new technology of eliminating criminals by high voltage electricity but rather on those whose destiny clearly pointed in that direction. He became determined to develop and prove his theory that the evil expressed by violent, maniacal conduct originated with an abnormality in the brain which was compounded and triggered by external stimuli. The excitement of the Columbian Exposition of 1893 was a milestone event along these lines as it was the first recorded emergence of what is now known as the "serial killer." As this great world's fair in Chicago progressed, which Monti participated in as a technical consultant, a deranged madman named Dr. H. H. Holmes was murdering numerous people mere blocks from the event. His evil crimes were eventually discovered and he was executed by the hangman on May 7, 1896. Aside from this event, murders were generally believed to be the product of lust, greed or anger.

* * *

A daily trip to Sing Sing by horseback and ferry was simply too time consuming and arduous to be practical, so Monti took a room in a local roadside inn while returning to Tuxedo Park on weekends. He arranged with Warden Jenkins to spend time with various criminals, who were waiting on death row at the penitentiary for the next available seat in Old Sparky. At this time the delay in some of these executions became quite lengthy for multiple reasons. The age old methods of execution were either by hanging or firing squad. However, some considered these to be too barbaric and began lobbying the governor for a more humane method. With the recent technological advances in electrical science, Edison, and others experimented with and developed the electric chair in response. The lives of many dogs, horses, pigs and other animals were sacrificed for these ghoulish tests. Some still complained that electricity was also inhumane and electrical technicians still needed to develop details such as the proper voltage and the optimal method of transmission to the body to satisfy the naysayers. So, the executions were delayed through a series of fits and starts providing Monti with time to interview and analyze a number of the most heinous murderers in Sing Sing.

His first study was a clever madman named McGrath, who was bestowed with the sobriquet: "The Slicer." Slicer McGrath earned his jolly nickname for the habit of taking fine slices of flesh with a straight razor from the faces of his trussed-up victims before he'd end the entertainment by slitting their throats. Upon discovery, many of the victims' heads were flayed clear to the bone.

Despite his derangement, McGrath was a very intelligent person, this contrast fascinated Monti, all the more. Upon his first meeting with the Slicer in the prison's dungeon-like death row cell, the warden had the Slicer secured in a straightjacket. He had the habit while incarcerated of attempting to use his teeth on anyone who earned his dislike, as a straight razor was unavailable. So the straightjacket was a necessary precaution. The two made for a bizarre looking pair with the unshaven murderer trussed-up in a laced canvas wrap as Monti sat opposite smoking his long pipe, notebook in hand, and wearing his pith helmet. Considering the proximity of his interviewees, he was even permitted to retain his knobkerrie.

Initially the Slicer remained mute with only an occasional grunt or growl emanating from him. But the probing questions which Monti raised began to interest McGrath. "What was the purpose of removing the flesh off your victims' faces?"

"They were my study cases, not my victims."

"Your study cases?" "Yes" responded McGrath in a low, monotone voice, "I was looking for their souls. The poets claim the eyes are the window into the soul, not so. It's through facial expression and if you remove the skin you may find the soul."

"You and I have similar curiosities, I too am interested in learning about the soul, however, I approach it in a different manner. In your research with five victims, no, I mean *study cases*, have you found any souls?" "Unfortunately this prison has curtailed my investigations." And in an ominous tone he stated, "But I assure you, I will soon continue."

Over the four interviews, Monti became vexed with his analysis of McGrath. Here he found a brutal, cold-blooded killer who was clearly deranged. But he was also very intelligent. He was articulate, shared the same interest and belief in the metaphysical mysteries that motivated people of faith, yet, he showed no empathy for those he horribly mutilated and murdered or for the lawlessness of his actions. How could he not see the conflict in his actions? Unfortunately, before Monti could delve further into the depths of the Slicer's logic, time ran out for McGrath and he was finally introduced to Old Sparky.

The next study for Monti was a murderer who killed her husband and children. She was a totally different character than McGrath. Unlike McGrath she was governed by total insanity with no spark of intelligence.

* * *

Monti was anxious to end his stay at the inn each week and welcomed his return to the Park each Friday night. Comfortably ensconced in his tower laboratory he would compile his voluminous notes, collating by the individual characteristics of the eight criminals he interviewed over the many weeks. He also spent time with both Warden Jenkins and the death row guards to supplement his own observations. His ultimate goal was to isolate any commonalities across the interviewees pertaining to their thinking and motivations then see if any conclusions could be drawn.

Late one Friday night, as the driving rain and high winds pummeled the slate roof above his lab, Monti, while wearily transcribing his notes from the week heard a loud crash on the circular stone stairway below. Jones was off in town for the night and Sinbad was lying at his feet, so the mansion below was, or should have been unoccupied. Fearing an intruder, he secured his Webley revolver from the desk drawer and slowly crept down the dark stairway aided by the dim light of an oil lamp. As he reached the bottom, a tall figure sprang from the shadows striking him across the head with a heavy object, knocking Monti to the floor. In a dazed condition, lying prostrate and up on one elbow, Monti raised his revolver and fired at the tall silhouette standing above him. As the shot rang out and reverberated in the dim, confined space, he fell back unconscious.

three

As usual, Jones arrived at the mansion at 7 a.m. and prepared Monti's morning repast, while expecting the squire to be working in his laboratory. As he entered the tower well, he dropped the tray in shock seeing the crumpled form on the stone floor. Losing the usual composure with his standard inquiry of: "And what may we be doing Sir?" He now anxiously shouted out, "Sir, Sir! What the deuce ever happened?" As he lifted the limp form, he heard a mumbled sound of pain emanate from Monti. "Jones, Jones, is that you?" Monti's head and shoulders were bathed in semi-dried blood with a large flap of skin hanging from the back of his head. Lying on the floor next to him was a heavy fireplace poker.

Monti, while holding a mirror, coached Jones as he attempted to suture the hanging flesh back into place after bathing his head. "Well Sir, how do we account for this? Has Sinbad ambushed you on the stairs as that nasty feline did to me?" "No, this was the work of a very nasty, non-feline on two, not four legs. We must inspect the stairwell for any clues as to just who this nasty cat was!"

After the make-shift medical repairs, they discovered a few drops of blood leading out to the rear terrace, then lost any trail in the adjacent garden. Monti now realized that he personally, was the target of a malevolent being, perhaps just as dangerous as those he had been studying. Starting with the death of poor Sara Mills, he believed the other Park deaths were no accidents of nature either. Over the past months he continually pestered the constable and other Park residents to pursue these events as crimes. This attempt on his life was evidence of just how right he was, and the fiendish killer was getting worried.

Learning from his Sing Sing investigations, Monti realized his enemy could be a very smart and yet sinister individual. Clearly the killer had the cunning to conceal his dirty work through a number of homicides by wrapping it in a cover of normalcy.

To yet again alert the naïve residents of the Park of the danger within their midst, he called a meeting of the Park elders at the Tuxedo club. He also invited the constable and town judge.

Saturday night, October 1, 1899.

"Thank you all for attending this evening. I wish to discuss the unprecedented number of deaths that have occurred recently within the Park. Starting with our friend and neighbor, poor Sara Mills, that vibrant, and kind young lady who was taken down in the prime of her life and two other fine citizens of this community, young Tommy Baxter and Mr. Jim Walker. All three lives have been lost—regardless of your thoughts—due to a peculiar, improbable and very suspicious set of circumstances. I believe we are in great danger."

Standing on the stage with his head swaddled in bandage, Monti continued:

"Only last night I was attacked and rendered unconscious in my own home! I submit to you all, there is an evil force lurking in this community and preying upon our citizens!"

The crowd immediately gasped and began a series of heated chatter amongst themselves. One shouted "Prove it!" Others "This is ridicules, he's crazy!" One elderly gentleman spoke for many in the crowd, "Mr. Montague-Smith, you perceive a mystical basis for every ill event that could befall anyone. Just last year when old man Thomas was kicked in the head by his horse, you suspected a chemical was involved and called for an investigation. Why, if it were up to you, you'd enlist a soothsayer every Ides of March and I'll bet you even try to turn base metal into gold in that laboratory of yours!" This last comment elicited laughter and a loud round of applause from the crowd.

Quincy stood in the background, drink in hand, egging on the naysayers.

In frustration, Monti, turned to the judge and constable appealing: "Look, last night I was attacked and nearly killed. I think I shot the attacker but barely hit him before fainting. The minimal blood trail indicated just a glancing hit so he is still lurking out there. There is definitely danger stalking this community. All I'm asking is to be permitted to conduct a detailed investigation of some of these events."

The judge looked at the constable, paused and then turned to Monti. "Look, I'll authorize an investigation on two counts. One . . . the constable must be involved, and two, you are not to pester people or intrude unnecessarily in people's privacy. You also must report everything you are involved with to me each week, and if you violate any of my orders, I'll have Constable Dillon place you under arrest, despite your reputation. Is that clear? And if you think you can go around this community shooting people, well, you had better have a real murderer in your sights and be able to prove it!"

With a firm voice and steely gaze, Monti responded with a determined, "Thank you judge."

Sunday morning, October 2, 1899.

As most Park residents were attending Mass at St. Mary's, plant operator, Gus Johnson arrived for his shift at the Tuxedo Park powerhouse. The powerhouse was a coal-fired, steam plant that used the Ramapo River for cooling water. The machine offered the Park's residents one of the first central station electric plant services north of New York City. It was Johnson's job to monitor the operating plant during the weekend peak load. His first job upon arriving was to check the steam pressure, output voltage and frequency.

The plant's generator was driven by a 100 horsepower Corless steam engine. The power transmission was via a twelve-ton, thirteen foot diameter flywheel close-linked to the generator. The huge flywheel projected down into a well in the concrete floor to accommodate its large size, which spun at sixty revolutions per minute.

As Johnson entered the whirring noise of the powerhouse and bent over the flywheel's shaft to oil one of the lubrication cups, a large figure stealthily crept from behind and pushed him into the well. He instantly became entangled in the spokes of the whirling mass as the huge cast-iron wheel mangled his body and tossed the bloody corpse across the floor. Not even a fraction of a cycle per second in the machine was lost to the puny resistance of his body. His mangled and bloody form laid on the powerhouse floor until the next shift change as the colossal machine continued powering the Park.

* * *

Word of this latest tragedy travelled through the Park almost immediately once the grisly remains of Johnson were discovered. Now, even Monti's detractors, those who all along simply considered him a wealthy and brilliant crackpot began to fear what may have descended upon them. They began to realize this latest death, occurring the day after Monti's warning to the community, was simply too coincidental to be a random event. It almost seemed as though they were being taunted by evil while Monti was being challenged.

His first task was a thorough investigation of the powerhouse. The great force of the rotating flywheel and the distance it pitched the body imposed such massive trauma that Monti was unable to determine if Johnson was assaulted before his engagement with the machine. However, he didn't believe for a moment the death was caused by accident. The floor was dry and Johnson was a very experienced plant operator. Besides, his lubricating task did not in any way expose him to the rotation of the machine. There simply was no clue to be found.

Monti realized the only way to proceed with any hope of successfully discovering the murderer was to start from the beginning with the murder of Sara Mills and analyze in detail every nuance of her death as well as the others. He believed a step by step process held the best probability of exposing a pattern and anyway, no one really investigated any of the deaths in a detailed manner before. So, maybe something unexpected may surface.

Hopefully, this plan would present results rather than wait for the murderer to stumble when striking again. Although Monti realized that the entire community was now aware that he had official sanction to investigate the cases, the murderer knew also. Being assaulted before, Monti now began carrying his Webley revolver everywhere, along with his knobkerrie and pipe.

His next step required the judge's approval to exhume Sara's body.

"But why must you autopsy the body? She's been dead close to two years and certainly much of her corpse must have deteriorated" commented the judge.

"Yes, this is true, but nonetheless it must be the first step in the investigation." The judge finally assented over the apprehensions of the pesky constable.

On a cold and rainy October morning Monti, the constable and two grave diggers lifted Sara's coffin from the ground. To the group's surprise, when opened, the box revealed a nearly intact corpse. The shady, cold soil of the church's cemetery, which was located at the top of a hill under a cropping of trees must have kept the body relatively cool and dry over the months, retaining nearly all of her flesh. Even her clothing was intact with her face expressing a sad, waxy composure.

Once again, Monti meticulously began to pick over Sara's body. He was amazed to see how well preserved she was despite her eternal sleep beginning almost two years before. He dutifully recorded in a log book, each of his every moves. Despite the morbid work, Jones attempted to assist. After pouring over her externally with a magnifying glass, Monti gently removed her clothing for later detailed analysis under his microscope. He purposely avoided lighting a fire in the laboratory's fireplace to keep the body cold, and in mid-autumn his lab was adequately cold.

Monti was extremely anxious to analyze the head for investigation of the region where the blood originally appeared in her nostril. He deftly removed her facial skin and muscle with his scalpel and then noticed, within the back of the nasal passage, a black, circular crust that he knew to be the remnants of dried blood. He sawed a small section of bone below her right eye, exposing the Perpendicular Plate of Ethmoid, the thin bone that supports the Septum Cartilage. "Viola! Just as I originally suspected, she was murdered with a thin, sharp instrument inserted into her brain by passage through her nostril!"

Jones, holding a handkerchief to his nose, was about to faint. "Sir, may we desist from this ghastly enterprise." Following that plea, Jones began to sink to the floor.

Armed with his positive proof establishing the murder of Sara, Monti was anxious to meet with both the constable and judge.

The constable rode up on his black mare just as Monti was entering the judge's house. "Well Doctor Montague-Smith, what have you discovered now, Jack the Ripper?" Monti simply brushed-off this sarcastic greeting, commenting, "I think . . . you will find my 'discovery' quite interesting."

Monti entered into a detailed dissertation of his findings for the fascinated jurist and the confused, bored lawman: "To begin with, I was pleased to find the body of Sara Mills almost perfectly intact, I presume due to the dry, cool environment of the churchyard. The flesh was not totally supple, nor was it desiccated, in fact, it was perfectly preserved for just what I was looking for."

Addressing the judge, Monti continued: "When we first discovered Sara's body, I detected a faint odor of chloroform around her face and I noticed a redness or irritation around the nose. Particularly interesting and telling was a small amount of blood ringing the inside of her right nostril, continuing into the nasal canal. At the autopsy, the nostril still contained the remnants of dried blood. Naturally, the skin was no longer flush nor was there any lingering odor of chemical; much subtlety dissipates over time in the cold earth. Due to the evidence of blood, without any outward sign of trauma to the face, I dissected her right cheek region, through the nose flesh and cheek bone and discovered the intrusion of a three millimeter diameter hole, parallel to the nose cartilage and through the thin bony structure behind the eye that separates the sinus from the brain."

"And what doctor, does this prove besides a corpse that had hay fever?"

"My dear constable, this proves that she was murdered by the insertion of a very sharp, long, thin instrument into her nostril and then into her brain, killing her instantly. Perhaps a rod of some sort, or maybe an icepick. The diabolical beauty of this is that death is immediate, soundless and there is very little blood released from the brain. If it were not for the faint chemical odor, and minute appearance of blood, her death would appear perfectly normal!"

The judge shook his head in bewilderment, "Doctor, please continue."

"The scenario is this, Sara was abducted from her home just before the Autumn Ball was starting. The killer entered through the French doors in the library, probably crept-up from behind and used a chloroform cloth on her face, which would depress the nervous system and render her helpless, then half dragged the limp body to the lake shore and rowed across to the colonel's boathouse. This was the killer's target destination, knowing that, (a) the dock is long, therefore, adequately separated from the house so as not to be heard, and, (b) the colonel and his wife would be at the ball. In the boathouse he simply had all the time he wished to perform his evil deed. One outstanding, loose end: we interviewed the entire manor staff and all were cleared, except the butler."

"Well why not man!" Monti, casting a side glance at the constable said, "Judge, as you saw, the community disbelieved anything except a natural cause for the explanation of the death." Dillon exhaled a slight sigh of relief for being let off the hook for his original criticisms and all of a sudden became very officious exclaiming "Well, we had better go and arrest that butler immediately!"

"Not so fast constable, you remember, motive and proof must be established before we have a murderer. Doctor, was she sexually abused?"

"No judge, there was no evidence of sexual molestation. In fact, she was still chaste."

"Well why . . . but how could anyone be so evil to wish to destroy such a beautiful creature in the prime of her life? Why, in my years on the bench, I've never, not with the robbers, or drunks, or even brutal husbands . . . have I seen this type of senseless crime! Not even in war. We must track down this monster!"

"I know it seems puzzling, judge, but I've learned that there is pure evil in the world beyond the normal mind to comprehend. There are those, and thank the stars very few, but there are those, who, in their own demented minds find justification and even pleasure in the suffering of others."

* * *

The first order of business was to interrogate the butler. Despite Dillon's insistence of arresting him on the spot, he had a solid alibi. They followed-up in town with a woman who had a long term relationship with him. On that night the butler and his lady took the train to Long Island to attend the rage of the season, the popular Buffalo Bill Wild West Show and they even had the cancelled ticket stubs to boot.

Although just as cold as the Sara Mills case, Monti was directed—with the strong encouragement of the judge—to investigate the other mysterious deaths that occurred over the past months within the Park.

Monti knew that a detailed analysis of the other murder victims would be fruitless. Young Tommy Baxter died under what appeared to be natural causes. Exhuming his body to study what may be remaining of a scalp wound, if remaining at all, probably wouldn't establish anything. And besides, he was in the ground too long to determine if any water remained in his lungs which would indicate drowning rather than severe head trauma. Also, his mother was still too distraught to suggest an exhumation of the body. Pursuing details of the other murders would be just as useless.

As Monti planned his next move, the Park settled in to a state of organized fright. The usual round of afternoon cocktail parties, golf dates and picnics ended. Even the bar at the Tuxedo Club closed early and the usual attendees accompanied each other home in groups; all carried firearms.

With an enormous surge of emotion, Monti was determined to pursue the deranged killer, but also continue his investigations at Sing Sing, however, only on a part-time basis. He took some comfort in knowing he'd be out of reach of the killer at least part of the time, except on his terms, for he was convinced that he was the next target.

four

Monti's plan now was twofold: continue his studies at the prison, but at a reduced rate in the hope of detecting a possible similarity in mindset between the derangement of those incarcerated and the Park's murderer, and when back in the Park, present himself as bait to the murderer on a planned and organized basis, on his ground. Consequently, he reduced his stay at the inn to three days a week while the other days he would expose himself in an obvious manner in the Park.

J.T.

The hostelry contained an intriguing group of boarders. Most were in law enforcement, associated with the prison; state troopers, sheriffs or lawyers representing the incarcerated.

When taking his dinner one evening in the inn's dining room, Monti noticed the most intriguing of all the guests, a very comely young woman sitting at a table opposite him. He was taken back by her stunning blue eyes and her long red hair. She also spied him and wondered at his unique appearance of tweed jacket and vest with pith helmet lying on the chair beside him as he puffed on a ridiculously long pipe. As all the other diners wore conventional business suits, he looked to be a lost hunter just in from the African bush veld.

After a few minutes, his interest could no longer be contained and rose to introduce himself, but upon moving from the table he stumbled over a chair pitching his pipe into the air and pith helmet to the floor. Some of the burning embers managed to land in the lady's lap. In a fit of embarrassment, Monti began to brush the sparks from her dress but then thought better than to place his shaking hands on her person.

"Oh my dear lady, I'm, I'm so sorry!" She immediately stood up brushing herself off in a state of hilarious laughter. As the crowded dining room patrons looked on in startled silence, Monti blurted out "Please accept my apology!"

"Oh, it was nothing. Are you injured?"

"Why, no. Are you burnt?"

"No I'm fine. Perhaps you should sit down for a moment." She said with an engaging smile.

At that offer, Monti retrieved his pipe and helmet and pulled up a chair. He sat down. "Whew, that was quite a trip you took!"

"Yes, it certainly was. My name is Montigue-Smith" as he extended his hand. "I'm Carolyn Samuels, but my friends call me Carrie. Are you here for the prison?"

"Yes, I'm visiting for some research, and most call me Monti."

"Aha, I'm also here for research . . . Monti. What type of work are you doing?"

"Well, I'm studying some of the death row inmates to determine why they have committed their crimes."

"What a coincidence! I'm here for a similar reason. I'm on sabbatical from Columbia College to write a book on some of the murderers here and their motivations. Some think their derangement is the result of their upbringing and I tend to agree."

"Are you a medical doctor?" Monti questioned.

"No, not really, not yet. I'm studying for my Doctorate in Psychiatry. Are you?"

"Well, I have university schooling in medicine but I'm also an engineer. The two seemingly disparate disciplines are complementary as they offer a bit of a different slant on subjects like capital crime. On the one hand, insight into the physical effects on the victim, and on the other, technical analysis of the local environment of the crime."

"And what's your theory on the driving force behind murderous intent?" Carrie inquired.

"Since I'm investigating those who commit a string of individual murders over time, without any obvious connection to the victims, there is no clear motive such as personal, gain, or overt anger, or other of the logical motives for taking a life. So I believe there must be a major character flaw, or a biological anomaly within the brain or a combination of the two that compels the murderer."

"Well, I'm not so sure it's as complicated as that. I think living in total poverty and lacking an education may drive someone to extreme levels of jealousy and hatred."

"Granted, this may have a bearing, but I don't think it's the full story, Carrie."

"Carrie, perhaps we could compare our findings." Monti commented with a twinkle in his eye. "After all, the similarities in our work could develop into a synergetic relationship" he mused half tongue in cheek, as he looked at the ceiling.

At first, Carrie was taken back by the suggestion of "relationship." She was always skeptical of entering into personal relationships with men, particularly with a man as eccentric and unknown as this stranger. However, she clearly recognized his brilliance and was somewhat intrigued by his overt peculiarities.

The next afternoon the two researchers met in the inn's dining room; Carrie with her manuscript and Monti with his log.

* * *

Monti began by reviewing the past events in the Park, the gory details of the murders and the initial disbelief of the Park residents that such heinous crimes could occur within their idyllic community. Monti also provided a brief biography of himself, his many travels and quirky interests.

Carrie was well aware of the famous upscale Tuxedo Park and its moneyed inhabitants. She also understood the arrogant, self-centered attitude that seemed to define many wealthy people. Carrie originated from a much more modest background. Her father was a middleclass shop owner in New York City who early on recognized the precociousness of his young daughter. Winning a scholarship while in high school enabled her to attend

Colombia College. There, she developed a curiosity for delving into the human spirit and was greatly influenced by writings of the great Sigmund Freud.

"Monti, just how do you expect to find the killer?"

"As impractical as it may sound my dear, through study and exposure. That is, by determining what makes him tick and baiting a trap."

"How can you trap him if his killings are so random, a young woman, a young boy, then a stable hand and a plant worker. All at different times and locations and in different manners?"

"Carrie . . . granted there is no pattern for his treachery, his victims are targets of opportunity. His lust for killing seems to be satiated for a period of time and then he strikes again when the excitement wears off. Regarding a trap, I don't know yet. I'm sure he knows I'm on his trail and he will try for me again at the next opportune time. So, I simply need to make myself available."

"Make yourself available! Why, you'll be a sitting duck!"

"No. Not if I expose myself at a time and place of my choosing with the location under my control, and *that* is what I have yet to figure out."

His self-imposed three day stay at the inn was nearing an end and he needed to return to the Park, so he asked Carrie if she would be returning to the inn the following week.

"Of course, I still have much work to prepare for my manuscript. But, but, are you leaving today?"

"Yes, I'm taking the evening ferry so I'll be available first thing in the morning."

"Have you developed your plan for a trap?"

"No, not yet, that's why I want to have a fresh start in the morning."

In a high-pitched, urgent voice, Carrie blurted out, "Well, can I go with you?"

"Go with me, of course not! One, it will be too dangerous for you to associate with me in the Park, you'll stand out like a sore thumb. And two, I don't need to worry about you as I will certainly be worrying about myself."

"But I could be a big help. An extra set of eyes will be helpful, and besides, I may notice clues that, despite your insights, may elude you."

Actually, Carrie's interest had self-serving motives. This would be a wonderful addition to her book, the actual firsthand tracking of a murderer, and besides, she was becoming infatuated with Monti.

"How could I justify bringing you back to the Park out of the clear blue? It would be improper and the Park's gossiping set would have a field day, not to mention the danger. And besides, if you stayed at my place, your reputation would be scandalized."

"Well, I have truly become your professional colleague and is there a local hotel where I could stay?"

"I guess you could board at the club."

Monti realized that his interest in Carrie was becoming much more than just a professional curiosity—he was falling in love. Against his better judgment he conceded to her wish. His feelings were such that he despaired at the thought of departing without her.

They returned their rented horses at the ferry terminal in Westchester County and secured a buggy on the west bank of the Hudson for the trip to Tuxedo Park. The ferry trip and the two hour ride through the forest provided time to plot their next move. When checking into the club, Monti, accompanied by the stunning redhead, generated shocked chatter and raised an endless round of lewd speculation among the usual patrons at the bar—one of the many of Monti's concerns. No doubt the sudden emergence of him being accompanied by a gorgeous woman would imme-diately filter through the Park, the killer would also learn.

The following morning, Monti took Carrie on a tour of the Park and his mansion. She was most impressed by his tower laboratory and strangely, by Jones. However, Jones did not share the same admiration. While around Carrie, Monti detected an air of arrogance in Jones, perhaps originating from him recognizing her lower class background. But actually, Jones instinctively detected the growing bond between Carrie and Monti and developed a degree of jealousy.

Monti was anxious to introduce Carrie to the judge, who instantly developed a fondness for her. On meeting the constable, she later described him as being "creepy" to which Monti had a hearty laugh.

"You know Carrie, in his prime, he was quite a policeman. He was with the Pinkertons during the War Between the States, and developed quite a reputation tracking down rebels. Some even say he was on the detail that captured John Wilkes Booth."

"I don't care, he's still creepy."

As the days passed, all seemed quiet in the Park. They spent their time in the laboratory, and evenings at the club or attending various social events. Monti was always careful to ensure they were at events where there were large groups of people, and naturally, he always carried his trusty Webley revolver. He also instructed Jones to carry his broom handled Mauser, which he wore in a shoulder-holster, at all times, despite its bulk.

J.T.

One afternoon in the lab, while comparing notes on the criminal mind, Monti strained with a severe headache. Since suffering the blow on his head from the mysterious intruder, he began developing occasional, throbbing headaches. Carrie insisted on applying a damp, cool compress to his forehead.

Staring into her eyes as she held the cloth to his head, he gently grasped her wrist and drew her near to him. As their bodies touched, he gently pressed his lips to hers. She instantly encircled his shoulders, pressing her mouth hard against his mouth as she pressed her torso to his. After a few moments of this intense embrace, he quietly whispered into her ear:

"Carrie, I have never felt this way before as I do towards you! Day and night, you constantly occupy my thoughts. You brighten my days as your absence darkens my nights. I love you deeply and must have you forever!"

"Oh Monti, I . . . I think I have the same feelings toward you, but we barely even know each other! We don't even know if this is just a fleeting infatuation!"

"Carrie my love, I know my own mind and feelings. I have thought about this for days and would never express so openly and honestly to you if I were not sure of my love. Please tell me you feel the same way."

At stating this, he held her body closer to him as she squeezed her arms tighter.

"Oh Monti, I . . . I think I feel the same way about you, but, but, we must be sure."

Just then, a gentle knock on the door followed by Jones announcing tea time. This intrusion broke the embrace of the startled pair and the tender moment was immediately lost.

"Sir, would you and the lady care for your afternoon repast?"

"Yes Jones, please enter."

The heavy door opened and Jones entered carrying a silver platter with teapot, cups and saucers along with assorted pastries. After placing down his burden, Jones exited.

"Monti, he is an interesting character, and wearing that pistol, he appears all the more extraordinary!"

"Yes, I agree. He is no more unique than his employer!"

"Well, your uniqueness is one of the traits that initially caught my attention, besides the near disaster of catching a lap full of burning pipe embers!"

"OK, OK, enough of my masculine charm. But Jones is an extraordinary man, in fact, I owe my life to him."

"Oh Monti, please tell me!"

"I was serving as a young subaltern with the British Army in the Northern Transvaal in Africa during the outbreak with the Boers. We had fought our way up to the top of a bloody pile of rocks called Majuba Hill. That was back in 1881, oh, seems like ages ago. It was a bad move where we were. We spent the night there out in the open and in the morning the Boers began moving up the hill. We had cover but they were better shots. As our men began to get hit, they panicked and began a mad dash down the hill, many who weren't shot, fell to their deaths.

"I jumped up and tried to stop the rout when I got hit; I fell like a dropped log. A young corporal picked me up and began carrying me down the hill until he got hit. I hit the ground a second time and the corporal again picked me up and under intense fire managed to carry me down the hill to safety. That was Jones for you, he was a jolly brave chap!

"After that we both spent time in the hospital and, due to our injuries, we were then cashiered out of the army."

"What did you do then?"

"Well, I was always fascinated with the Zulus and wanted to study them. So Jones and I partnered and journeyed to Natal to live with them for a spell. After a couple of years in South Africa with the natives, exploring and doing some sport hunting, my father contacted me with a proposition to move to America. Jones accompanied me and we remained together, ever since."

"He seems so, so, deferential towards you."

"He has managed to retain both the officer—enlisted man relationship common within the army rankers in addition to the British attitude of a servant towards his lord. And thank goodness he never adopted the casual approach to aristocracy prevalent here in America! However, I do really owe so much to him, more than I can ever repay."

Monti and Carrie began spending blissful days together, horseback riding through the Park and evening dinners at the club. One of their favorite pastimes was boating on the lake. Monti kept a small, sail-rigged skiff on which he taught her to sail. One day as he tightened the mainsail against the gentle breeze, Carrie mused,

"Monti dear, what do you think the future holds for us?"

"The first order of the day is to clear up this dastardly business plaguing the Park, and it will not be easy! I feel quite guilty with not having yet solved this puzzle."

Attempting to lighten the conversation, she responded, "Well, following all of this, maybe we could assist each other with our interests. I wish to finish both my book and medical degree and you have numerous scientific puzzles to solve. I think we could be a big asset for each other!"

"Yes my love, after we weather this storm, my main pursuit in life will be to make you happy! All other activities will be secondary—whatever makes you happy will be my goal."

five

The club was all a tither in anticipation of the coming Tuxedo Thoroughbred Championship Race. No single sporting event held more importance than race week. The famous event began by P. Lorillard when he acquired Hunters Luck, a fine thoroughbred, grade II mare when on a trip to Kentucky years ago. Following those early days, the race had attracted some of the finest racehorses in the country, and Tuxedo Park believed it was home to the best.

The seven and a half furlong, dirt track was located in the middle of the Park, complete with canopied stands, paddock, tack room and stables. The week before the event was a confusion of endless rounds of cocktail parties, decoration hanging and the chaos of numerous visitors with horses in tow scrambling into the club for lodgings. This was just the type of event that troubled Monti, one where an evil doer can easily move throughout the mayhem, undetected. He realized also, that it could present the best opportunity for the murderer to tip his hand.

Regarding the upcoming week, Monti began to crystalize a plan for Carrie.

"Carrie darling, I have a thought, we must take advantage of race week. I think it may offer an opportunity for us to flush-out our quarry. Consider the many lawn parties, the club dinner-dance and the many other events held that week, not to mention the race itself. Large crowds will be out and about both day and night . . . the perfect environment for our murderer to attempt striking."

"Yes my love, but you may very well be his quarry and in the confusion you will be terribly exposed."

"It may be our best chance, but my biggest worry is for you, not myself."

"Monti, how can you and I expect to oversee the numerous crowds on race day? And besides, before and after the race, the people will be dispersed all over the Park, and that's not to mention the days leading up to the race!"

"Well, you're right. We'll need to enlist others."

"But who? And who can we trust?"

They both realized they were woefully incapable of handling the task at hand so their next move was to meet with the judge and Constable Dillon to strategize a plan.

The judge called out and enlisted selected and trusted members of the fire brigade along with certain members of the club, all were sworn in as deputies by Dillon and directed to carry concealed firearms for the next few days. They were divided into teams of two, all sworn to secrecy and directed to casually conduct themselves in their normal manner. During the days leading up to the race, the club members would be the only teams, along with Monti, Carrie and the constable patrolling within the Park. By tradition and due to elitism, the town folk were never allowed to socialize within the Park's gates and were excluded from entry to the club at all times except as hired help. Their casual presence within the Park the week before the race would raise suspicion if not outright, angry complaints by the Park's Brahmins. So the majority of the deputized were absent the week preceding the race.

On race day, each team would be assigned to various stations within the racetrack periphery; some in the stands, some at the paddock, others along the track rail and a team in the stables. Monti and Carrie would post themselves at a high vantage point in the stands. With binoculars they would be able to pan a wide view of the entire venue. The constable would be a roving member of the group as the judge would take his honored place in a cordoned-off section of the stands reserved for dignitaries.

* * *

Monti and Carrie spent the days leading up to the big event socializing at many of the prerace cocktail and dinner parties. The latter 1890s was still steeped in the notion of Victorian virtue. While nonchalantly displaying her superior intelligence, some accepted Carrie simply as the eccentric Montague-Smith's professional colleague, particularly since she was discretely lodging at the club and not in Monti's mansion. The park residents, other than some engaged in lewd chatter between themselves regarding Carrie, mostly embraced her as one of their own. While the others joyfully speculated on her place in his personal life, believing her club residence was just a ruse to cover their illicit affair.

On the morning of the race, the owners, horse attendants and jockeys began preparing the thoroughbreds and themselves for the big event. The weather provided for a warm, beautifully sunny and windless day; perfect for the race. The teams of undercover sleuths began taking their positions at the track with Monti and Carrie joining many of the Park residents for breakfast on the club's veranda.

As one o'clock approached, the stands began filling in with throngs of people as the entire circumference of the oval track rail held back the public, three persons deep. The Park dandies were attired in finery reminiscent of the British swells at Ascot. The ladies wore newly fashionable, brightly colored, spring dresses and large, gaudy hats, the men donned top hats. Even Monti appeared wearing a top hat, sans his customary pith helmet.

As the gun went off, the throng of horses broke from the gate in a release of tightly restrained energy; their thundering hooves tearing up the turf in clumps and flinging it aside onto the rail and the feet of those standing nearby. The jockeys whipped their mounts with their riding crops in a frenzy of excitement. The standing crowd cheering in a roar, some even using a megaphone to encourage on, their own favored pick to win.

As the horses entered the backstretch, the third horse on the inside rail, number six, stumbled and hit the dirt at a lightning fast pace, turning three summersaults as it pitched its jockey high into the air. The crowd released a huge sigh of concern while the jockeys ahead fought with their reins to slow and stop their frightened mounts.

At once, those standing closest to the rail climbed over and ran to the prostrate forms lying on the track. Both horse and jockey were lying in a cloud of dust, dead.

Monti and Carrie immediately jumped down from the stands and ran to the track, pushing and shoving aside the crowd.

"Don't touch anything." He yelled as Carrie cried in shock when seeing the mangled body of the jockey. "Move aside, move aside." As those near the accident cleared a path, Monti knelt down next to the crumpled body of the jockey, momentarily placing his fingers on the jockey's neck hoping to sense a pulse. He then quietly announced the man was dead. Just then, as the judge and Dillon arrived, Monti stood and slowly paced around the form telling a man standing nearby to find a stretcher.

Monti then walked back to the horse and spent a few minutes analyzing the body. He then ordered some onlookers to grab the animal's legs and together they strained and turned the heavy beast over. Again, he analyzed the body, particularly the small bloody hole in the animals flank.

"The horse just seemed to stumble over his own feet!" Exclaimed the constable.

"No" responded Monti, "he was shot off of his feet. Judge, I want both the jockey and the horse brought to my laboratory." He told the constable to make the arrangements to "have the horse taken to my tower and placed below the large external door on the third floor, just below the overhead block and tackle. I need to autopsy both man and horse."

In the lab Monti immediately knew the jockey's death resulted from a broken neck upon hitting the ground. He knew the horse was a different story and was his real focus. With Carrie's assistance, he carefully removed the skin in the area of the bullet hole and tediously began removing flesh along the track of the wound. His interest was twofold: to remove the bullet and to determine the precise path of its travel.

In the morning, after a long night spent in the lab and at the racetrack, he and Carrie rode into town to inform the judge of their findings.

"Good morning your honor, we have some information we think you should know."

"And a good morning to you two, notwithstanding yesterday's tragedy. I certainly hope it will shed some light on these ghastly killings. The Park's residents are so frightened, half of them are threatening to move back to the city."

Monti began a detailed monolog on the autopsy's results in his usual pedantic manner:

"A gun shot clearly caused the event, the sound masked by all of the race commotion. The jockey died instantly upon hitting the ground, he suffered a broken neck. The horse is a different story. A bullet, a thirty caliber, military round entered his left flank and passed laterally into his midsection. This caused the horse to stumble and fall. Based upon the angle of the trajectory and the direction of the race, I would say the shooter was located south of the racetrack. Based upon the angle of the bullet's path within the horse, that is a dropping angle as the bullet came to rest three inches below the entry wound, I would say the shooter was a long distance from his target. The bullet was falling as it entered the horse. Indeed, the shooter was a fine marksman, perhaps located high in a tree behind the stands.

"I suggest we scour the ground for a spent cartridge case in the tree line to the rear of the stands."

"But why would someone look to shoot a horse during the race?" Questioned the judge as he shook his head in dismay.

"Judge, the horse was of no consequence to the shooter. He was interested in killing the jockey, the horse was simply an easier target to hit. The killer knew that at that speed, the chances of surviving a fall would be minimal. His motivation was no doubt twofold, to strike fear in the Park in a most dramatic manner while satisfying his lust for violence. We are dealing with the same deranged individual who committed the previous crimes."

"My word, we must track down this devil now! Please immediately contact the constable and explain all this to him. Would we be wise to call in the state police?"

"I don't believe that's advisable, judge. They wouldn't and couldn't do anything beyond what we could do. In fact, they would start all over from the beginning and waste a lot of time, a precious commodity that we simply can't tolerate. And besides, we know the Park, they don't."

"Do you think the culprit is a Park resident or someone from the outside?"

Monti pondered for a moment, "the probability is that he's either a resident or possibly one of the hired staff. One who knows the Park intimately and who frequents the Park. One who would not raise any suspicions by his continued presence."

"Why do we keep referring to 'him,' maybe it's a woman we should be after?" Carrie pondered.

"No, it can't be a woman. The average woman would not have had the strength to drag Sara Mills into the boat and then remove her into the boathouse. And the boot size was too big for a woman's foot. We will meet with the constable and inform him of my findings. We also need to search for any evidence around the track and behind the stands. I think we should immediately post a roving team of deputies to police the Park day and night."

* * *

When informed of the latest events, the constable was shocked and as usual, disbelieving of Monti's findings.

"Your claim of a sharpshooter being able to hit a moving target, even a horse at that distance is not realistic! It's simply too far. I think this was simply a tragic accident. Someone, a careless person, was no doubt off somewhere taking potshots and fired into the air. If, as you say, this was a military round, well, they can travel over a mile!"

"Yes, that may be true, but during the War Between the States, some sharpshooters were so skilled, they were able to hit targets at a great distance. And they were using antique weapons. More recently, we learned the same with the Boers. The papers are reporting that the new Mauser rifles being used in Cuba by the Spaniards are taking down our troops, sometimes at very long range. So I suggest we organize a search party to look for clues and end these useless speculations."

Once again the trusty fire brigade, still sworn-in with deputy status, was enlisted to canvas the entire area around the track and stands. As one team picked through the leaf covered duff behind the stands, a member of the brigade came running to Monti and Carrie with his hand in the air: "I found it, I found it!"

The young boy picked up a spent cartridge case below a large sugar maple tree. Monti immediately followed the boy to the location of the tree and began searching below its broad limbs. Impressed into the soft earth were boot prints of the type Monti originally discovered near the lake the night of Sara Mill's murder. The killer's struggle to reach the lower branch while climbing disturbed the leaves revealing the prints.

"Well now, just as I thought!" Monti then began to climb up along the branches. As he climbed higher he noticed dried soil deposited on some of the branches by the killer as he had climbed the day before. At a height of about thirty feet above the ground, the foliage opened, revealing a perfect view over the roof of the stands and beyond to the racetrack's backstretch. Besides the commanding view, the tree offered a convenient limb with which the shooter no doubt used as a rest to steady his rifle for the long shot. The ever incredulous constable was now forced to agree with Monti's claims.

The next few days were extraordinarily quiet in the Park as the residents hunkered down in the security of their mansions. Some even relocated back to their Manhattan townhouses for the safety and security that distance provided. Carrie continued her stay at the club, shuttling between only her room and the tower laboratory. She and Monti spent many hours poring over details of the murders, looking for any previously, unobserved clues. They both suspended their research trips across the river. The constable organized the fire brigade into a posse on a continually patrolling basis.

To reduce tensions, the judge convinced the club's board members to hold a party and dance on Friday night despite the pall that had descended upon the community.

A large contingent of the Park turned out for the event. When Monti and Carrie entered the ballroom, Quincy Mortimer Thompson immediately became entranced with the stunning redhead and flew to her side. He totally ignored Monti as he grasped her hand and gallantly brought it to his lips exclaiming:

"Well hello there, my name is Quincy, and what may you be named fair maiden?" She was taken back by this rude provocation and embarrassingly responded,

"Why, why, my name is Carrie, Carrie Samuels."

Monti just stood there and fumed as he was being totally ignored. He knew Thompson from the many past social events in the Park; he also knew of his notoriously philandering reputation. Monti always held in the highest esteem those he believed to be intelligent and productive individuals. Thompson's only productivity was in the realm of his shady indiscretions.

"Well my dear Carrie, your entrance has certainly brought dash and sparkle to our dull surroundings. We must get to know one another."

At that rude and insulting introduction, Monti grabbed Carrie by the arm and forcefully escorted her to the bar.

Through a haze of cigar smoke and loud chatter, she squirmed in Monti's tight grip exclaiming:

"Monti, you're hurting me!"

"I'm sorry, but that man is not the type you should be socializing with, he's a cad of the first class!"

"Well who is he?"

"He's simply a wealthy ne'er-do-well who was fortunate enough to have been born into money. An original thought or useful action has never emerged from his existence."

"He did seem quite forward, but also quite interesting."

"Well, it certainly would be in your best interest to avoid him."

"Oh Monti please, I can determine what's in my best interest. Do I detect a hint of jealously?"

"Of course not! It's just that we have enough to contend with, without associating with someone of his questionable reputation."

Carrie rolled her eyes and let the matter drop.

As the night wore on, Carrie became restless. Monti would not, and in fact, could not dance. Aside from the never-ending aches and pains he continually suffered from his war wounds and recent gunshot, he thought the act of dancing was a mindless and primitive ritual. It reminded him of the wild and senseless gyrations of the natives he left back in Africa.

The sly Mortimer Thompson took note of this. He sauntered over to where they sat, bowing and swinging his arm around in a circular motion like Sir Galahad when dropping his cape, and asked Carrie for a dance.

"My dear lady, will you honor me with the great pleasure of your presence on the dancefloor?"

Carrie was taken back by the unexpected request and Monti was struck dumb. In an effort to sound polite and sophisticated, she agreed and stood up before Monti could regain his composure. As they whorled about the floor, Monti's ever questioning mind began to hum:

This mountebank is a skilled polo player, routinely around horses. He frequently wears riding boots. I wonder what size and style. How can I make a casting?

After the dance he raised his speculation to Carrie.

"You know Carrie, Thompson is a keen horseman, no doubt owning many pairs of riding boots. I think I'll try to enter his stables and see about making a mold."

"Oh Monti, don't be silly! Just because he is courteous and has wonderful manners doesn't mean that he is a murderer. Just how many in the Park do you think own riding boots? And besides, how would it look if you were to be caught skulking around on his property? I do think you are jealous!"

"I am not jealous, I'm just trying to consider all possibilities. But you are probably right, he couldn't have hit that galloping horse at better than two-hundred yards. In fact, he's too effeminate to have ever used a gun."

* * *

Despite having their first spat, the next day all was forgotten.

"Monti, when will this nightmare ever end?"

"I don't know my love. I feel so helpless cooped-up here in the mansion while this vile scoundrel may be out stalking his next victim. We can't just sit here waiting. I must begin spending my time roving around the club, the golf course, and anywhere I can to be seen. Then maybe the murderer will tip his hand."

"But the danger!" Carrie responded in a scared, heartfelt voice.

"I'm sure that I'm his prime target if I'm available. In my absence, that is, if he can't reach me, he'll hit any random, easy, target. While I'm sequestered here, his distorted emotions will drive him elsewhere and we cannot permit any additional killings. At least, if he tries for me, I'll have a better chance to both survive and nail him, much better chance than the average person—for I understand him."

For the next week Monti became a prominent fixture around the Park while spending his evenings at the club's bar, shooting billiards and commiserating with the locals. He even became an obvious presence at the stables and spent afternoons riding the roads and many bridal paths in the Park on his horse. Carrie stayed in the mansion, looked over by Jones. The judge, although a brave man having served with distinction in the War Between the States was too old to actively participate in the hunt, he wisely avoided the Park.

* * *

One dark, stormy night as he was returning from the club, Monti noticed there was no light emanating from the mansion's large bow windows, even the tower windows were dark. He tethered his horse at the iron gate and slowly approached the dark, imposing mansion, gun in hand. One of the large oak doors was ajar as he crept into the entry hall. Not a sound was to be heard but the wind and driving rain pelting the windows, the tall statuary lining the hall cast eerie shadows as he lit an oil lamp.

He began to slowly and quietly move through the first floor rooms, the dining room, the study, and the drawing room until he arrived at the rear of the mansion overlooking the glass paned conservatory; he would check that later. As he approached the door leading up to the tower, he was only able to open it partway, it seemed jammed. With a heavy push, he entered and shockingly realized the body of Jones had been blocking the door. He was unconscious, bleeding heavily from the head with gun in hand. It appeared he was attacked from behind when he entered through the doorway in the same manner that Monti was ambushed. Monti knew, by Jones's drawn pistol, he must have been moving through the doorway in a defensive, cautious manner, however, his first concern was for Carrie.

He then began creeping up the winding stone stairway, his heart thumping like a trip hammer. The laboratory door was open as he scanned the dark interior. After searching throughout the large room, on the alert and ready to use his revolver, he could see he was alone. Upon lighting the oil lamp over his desk, there lying was a note that forced his palpitating heart to drop; it was a message from the murderer. The velum paper, ripped from the desk's large pad and printed in large block letters, stated:

I HAVE HER NOW!
IF YOU EXPECT TO SEE HER ALIVE
I WILL BE AT THE RACETRACK TOMORROW NIGHT AT 12
COME ALONE!!

Monti then raced down the stairs to attend to his faithful butler, Jones. After reviving Jones and bandaging his head, in the same manner as his missing love Carrie had recently nursed him, he began to question Jones.

"Sir, I seem to only have a hazy recollection of events. I, I, think I heard a loud noise on the stairs, and when I went to inquire . . . well, I don't actually remember what happened next!"

Horrific thoughts now raced through Monti's head. *Has he harmed her? Has she been defiled? It's all my fault, I never should have brought her here! I expected to be the target and now she is in the clutches of that evil demon.* He tried to block the lurid thoughts and concentrate on what must be done.

Informing anyone of the meeting was out of the question. He couldn't risk Carrie's life by violating the message's demand. Jones was the only one he could trust to participate in this dangerous mission. It was quite clear what the murderer planned, lure Monti into a trap where he would be killed, thereby eliminating his greatest threat.

"I must turn the tables Jones, and use this as a trap for this fiend."

"But Sir, how can you blindly walk into this without knowing where he will be lurking? The racetrack is a very large area, you can't just parade around in the open! And what of Miss Carrie?"

"Jones, I have no other choice but to expose myself, her life hangs in the balance. We must craft a plan that will minimize my danger as we maximize the killer's danger."

six

Monti and Jones spent the next day at the mansion brainstorming a plan for the dangerous operation ahead. As the murderer's note was vague on specifics, Monti knew the one option, while not knowing precisely where to go, was to openly walk the expanse of the racetrack area. This would expose him to the gun sights of a very skilled marksman which certainly was the killer's intent.
    J.T.

Another option, the safer one, was to lay in concealment and wait to see if the killer would expose himself and then spring upon him. This choice was the preferred tactic of Jones.

"Yes Jones, but the killer will surely know we are setting an ambush for him. This may very well sign a death warrant for Carrie."

"But you Sir, simply prancing about in the open will surely earn a bullet, and we well remember the last time we both earned bullet wounds! And besides, if you get killed, which you surely will if you expose yourself in the open, Miss Carrie will never be rescued."

After pondering this for a few minutes, Monti realized that lying in wait was the better of two poor options.

"Yes Jones, however we do it, we must stop him! This community has been paying the butchers bill for too long."

Monti studied the almanac and relying on his scientific acumen, learned that a full, clear moon would present itself that night.

"Jones, the moon will rise at 9:43, which means at midnight its azimuth over the horizon will only be forty-three degrees, and considering the trees, it will present long shadows, another impediment to us spotting him. I shall station myself at the far end of the track in the maintenance shed. You will adopt the killer's last modus operandi and post yourself in a suitably foliated tree, but closer to the track than the killer selected. Take the Mannlicher with you. Try to select a vantage point where you can provide good enfilade fire, and if he appears, try to only wound him! We must find Carrie.

"We need to be in position by nine p.m. before the moon rises, and stay deathly quiet moving in and thereafter and for the duration. We must be like hunters in a leopard blind. He will be lurking somewhere in the dark where he will have a good field of fire. If he doesn't show himself, we will remain in place until sunup and stealthily withdraw separately and regroup back here and plan our next move."

Later, as Monti quietly assumed his position in the maintenance shed, Jones crept about for a stout tree offering a good, angled view, diagonally across the track. His selection provided for a clear sweep of the entire expanse with the added advantage of a limb arrangement for both foot and rifle rest; a big advantage in quelling fatigue considering the time he may spend in wait. His 6.5, Mannlicher-Schoenaur rifle had a long tube telescopic sight with fine German optics, and Jones was a very good shot.

The night was eerily silent with the exception of the occasional hoot-hoot of a distant owl. As the moon began its track, it began to cast eerie, elongated shadows across the landscape that shortened as the orb arced to its zenith. Monti positioned himself near a partially propped-open window and continually checked his pocket watch as he fingered the hammer on his Webley revolver.

At midnight, all was quiet as a gentle breeze began to waft across the open track area, downwind from the direction of the shed. Monti took comfort in the thought of hunting man not animal regarding the movement of the breeze, although he did wish he could scent *his* prey. The hands on Monti's watch seemed to move at glacial speed: twelve-fifteen, twelve-thirty, twelve forty-five, one o'clock and yet no sign.

As the minutes ticked by, Jones thought he spied a slight movement from the corner of his eye. "Yes! It's him" Jones mumbled in a rush of adrenalin. A tall, dark form slowly began moving at the far end of the track. Jones slowly positioned his rifle while peering through the scope, he slowly clicked off the safety and placed the crosshairs slightly ahead of the movement and gently squeezed the crisp trigger. The crack of the high-velocity round reverberated across the track as Monti sprang from his hideout.

In his excitement, Jones fell the last ten feet from the tree. In a mad dash, both arrived at the approximate spot at the same time where Jones saw the figure. No one was there!

"I know I hit him! I know I hit him Sir!" as he knelt down and began to light a match. "No, no Jones, be careful. That light is just what the killer needs to take a bead on us. We'll wait around until daylight and then check around." At that they both walked over to behind the stands in the darkness and sat down to await the sun.

They both later returned to the spot and began studying the ground. After pacing around a few steps, Monti spied drops of blood. "Aha! You hit him alright! But not hard." After marking the location, they then began walking in a circular pattern to locate any blood trail, the same tracking tactic they would use after wounding an animal in Africa, many years ago. "So now the chase is on Jones, let's hope the blood continues." The intermittent drops pointed to the wood line. Even if the trail held out, this was a difficult and time consuming process. They continued into the woods for a hundred yards or so, trying to spot the occasional blood drop here and there on the leaf covered ground until the trail ended at a stream.

"Well now, he must have slopped along in the stream to throw any followers off the track."

"Shall we go right or left Sir?"

"We first start right for . . . let's say, a quarter mile. If nothing shows, we'll return here and try left."

They split apart, one on one side of the stream, with the other on the other side looking for any exit footprints and blood. After hours of tracking in vain, they gave up the chase and returned to the mansion.

Monti poured a tumbler of Scotch for himself and Jones, commenting,

"Well old friend, we failed with that one."

"I hope in our failure this scoundrel hasn't harmed Miss Carrie."

"No, he wouldn't, at least not yet. He also failed in his effort to kill me. As long as I'm alive, I believe he'll keep her safe. Carrie is his trump card in getting to me. Since his plan to lure me into the open did fail, I'm sure he'll contact me again. Now we must just sit and wait. However, I'll continue to stay in the open on the off chance he'll try to catch me off guard."

"Sir, people will begin to question about Miss Carrie's absence."

"Yes Jones, a good point. I will go to the club and spread word around that she returned to the prison to continue her research work for her book."

Monti returned to his former habit of horseback riding through the Park in the morning, and billiards at the club bar during the afternoon. As he entered the bar one day, the maître d' provided him with a sealed envelope. As he casually opened it and removed its contents he nearly fainted, it was from the murderer. The blood stained letter stated in the familiar block letters:

'So you think you escaped me! I watch you day and night. I could destroy you on horseback, or at the golf course, or shoot you when you go to the club. But, I hesitate, for I want your beautiful woman to see you die. If you expect her to live you MUST meet me at the powerhouse tomorrow night at 8. And if you plan a trick this time, your woman will bleed much more!'

The sight of Carrie's blood stunned Monti more than the ominous words and he stumbled into a chair to regain his composure.

* * *

The next morning as Jones answered a knock on the door, a courier handed him a note from the club in the form of a telegram. Carrie's father decided to travel to the park for a surprise visit with his daughter and would be staying at the club. He was scheduled to arrive today!

"Sir, Sir, whatever will we do! Her father's coming for a visit and his daughter has been abducted, and by a deranged murderer to boot! And you expect to rescue her tonight. Whatever will we do?"

As always, the Park had managed to keep its foibles and indiscretions from public view, so the papers were totally unaware of the murderous drama that had been unfolding within the Park. Consequently, her father was ignorant of the danger his daughter was being subjected to.

"We must meet him when he arrives, her father shall stay here."

"Sir, how can we conceal this horrible affair from him at the same time we're attempting to rescue his daughter?"

"Be realistic Jones, concealment from her father as we rescue his captive daughter, well, that's an impossible combination. We must take him into our confidence and hope for the best."

* * *

Mr. Samuels was a plump, aging businessman who struggled his way into the middleclass by his natural salesmanship talent. He had a keen mind and much energy. Carrie's mother had died in childbirth forcing Samuels to raise her on his own. This closeness forged a very tight relationship and an overbearing sense of responsibility in Carrie's father.

When he arrived at the mansion, Jones assisted Samuels in settling into his temporary abode. In late afternoon he joined Monti for cocktails on the veranda.

"So, Doctor Montigue-Smith, I've heard many complementary stories from Carrie regarding you, and incidentally, thank you for extending the hospitality of your home to me. I am very anxious to see Carrie."

"Please call me Monti, and Mr. Samuels, I have a very 'uncomplimentary story' to relate to you regarding Carrie."

"Alright Monti, and please call me Jake and what's this 'uncomplimentary story'?

Just then Jones returned with a fresh round of cocktails. Monti directed him to sit down.

"Jake, this is my assistant and friend, Jones." "I'm pleased to meet you Jones" responded Samuels as he extended his hand. Monti knew Jones was an important and very necessary part in the rescue of Carrie and wanted him to be an integral part of both the conversation and mission.

After a long pause and a sip of his drink, Monti began to tell the tale of past events to Samuels, "I know this is extremely dreadful to hear and consider, but you must understand all of the details."

As Monti began to recount the heinous acts leading up to the kidnapping of his daughter, Samuels jumped up from his chair, exclaiming, "Good grief man, are you saying my daughter is being held captive by a madman?"

"Yes sir, that's precisely what I'm saying."

"My heavens, we must go to the police at once!"

"I'm afraid that's not a good idea Mr. Samuels" commented Jones as he chimed into the conversation.

"You see Jake" as Monti began, "this madman, as you call him, is really not mad in the usual sense. In fact, he's very, very intelligent and that's the problem—a combination of a type of evil madness combined with brilliance. He's simply so cagey that we cannot enlist groups of people to pursue him. The police will simply get in the way and further jeopardize Carrie. Until now, that is before you arrived, Jones and I have been going it alone, and it must continue this way until he is destroyed."

"But, but, do you really expect me to sit here while my daughter is in great danger? Be assured, there is no possibility of that! I must participate! What time did you say the meeting is to take place? And just what did you say this maniac wants?

"My neck; at 8PM" responded Monti.

* * *

It was clearly evident there was no way to exclude Samuels from the eight o'clock caper. But he considered that maybe the feisty Samuels could be of use.

"This is the situation" Monti began. "The meeting location is at the powerhouse, which is located in a very isolated stretch of the Ramapo River. I will enter the generating hall through the main double doors and appear alone, so I will approach the building by myself; naturally I'll be armed. Jones, you enter the hall five minutes after me, very stealthily and bring your Mauser pistol, come into the hall from the single back door. Hopefully it will be unlocked. Jake, you will be posted fifty or so yards on the road leading to the powerhouse and remain out of sight with the Mannlicher.

"If we're lucky, I will engage the killer in talk and if I'm afforded an opportunity, I'll take him down. If not, Jones, you have a chance. Again, we must take him alive, remember, we must save Carrie!"

At the appointed hour they began to approach the building, however, unbeknownst to them, the lights in Tuxedo Park mysteriously went dark at seven thirty.

Monti slowly entered the generating hall carrying a hurricane lamp in one hand and his Webley in the other.

From the depths of the cavernous building he heard a deep, gravelly voice, "Well, the great Montigue-Smith has once again arrived for the rescue of the damsel in distress." The sound of the voice sounded falsely contrived, as though its owner was attempting to conceal just who was speaking.

"Well, if we are going to chat, at least present yourself like a gentleman" Monti rejoined.

"Ha ha, do you think I'm stupid enough to face you with a gun in your hand?"

At that, Monti bent down and placed the revolver on the concrete floor.

"Very good! Now step ten paces beyond it."

As Monti complied, a very tall figure stepped from the shadows at the end of the hall lighting an oil lamp as he slowly walked a few paces forward. The black figure had a heavy limp and wore a balaclava covering his face.

"I came as you directed, now where is Carrie?"

"Don't worry, there's time for that. So you think you could just shoot me down like a dog, eh? Your marksmanship is lacking, you only slightly grazed my leg."

"Is that why you're limping?"

"Don't get cocky! I still have both the lady and a gun on you."

"Where is she?"

"Ah yes, the reason you're so willing to walk into my trap. Hold up your lamp and walk to your left and you'll see her!"

At his direction, Monti began slowly walking and then let out a gasp shouting, "You devil! What have you done to her?"

In his vile voice the killer hissed, "Don't worry, she's still alive, only sleeping." Monti cast his eyes on Carrie, head down and spread-eagle with her arms and legs lashed to the iron spokes in the steam engine's huge flywheel. Immediately Monti reached up to check if she had a pulse. It was slow and faint but steady. The blackout in the Park occurred as the killer shutdown the steam engine to lash Carrie to the wheel.

"Don't attempt to cut her down or I'll start the plant operating at full speed." He ordered, as he slowly began to turn the hand wheel on the main steam stop valve. The heavy flywheel began to very slowly rotate carrying Carrie around with it. At full operating speed, the flywheel would turn at sixty revolutions a minute, which would spin Carrie in a whorl of death.

"Don't" Monti yelled as he stepped back from the machine. "Please close the valve! You can shoot me, I don't care. But release Carrie!" He pleaded. As the dangerous drama unfolded in the powerhouse, Jones was stymied outside by the locked rear door. In fear of endangering Monti and Carrie should she be inside, he just waited without breaking in, hoping to stop the killer if he came his way. Carrie's father, hunkered down on the road, was unknowing and unable to do anything.

"Well why don't you just shoot me and end all this?" Monti questioned.

"You fool, I'm enjoying the game too much! I don't want to kill you, you're my challenge! I intend to continue decimating the community as you continue to fail in catching me!" At that he closed the valve tight, bringing the slowing rotating wheel to a stop and ordered Monti to douse the hurricane lamp. In a moment he receded into the shadows and was gone.

Monti hurriedly found the matches in his pocket and relit the lamp. He cut the bindings on Carrie and gently lowered her to the floor as Jones finally broke down the rear door.

"My word Sir, what happened? I was unable to enter in fear of exposing you and Miss Carrie."

"Jones, get a lamp and bring Samuels in, then see if you can find that fiend."

After scouring the surrounding woods, the killer was nowhere to be found. Carrie was gently carried back to the mansion and revived from her chloroform induced sleep. Although dirty and disheveled, she was unharmed.

"Oh Carrie my darling, what has he done to you?"

"I'm alright father, he kept me bound and isolated but otherwise he left me alone."

"Carrie, did you see his face? Do you have any sense of who he is?" Monti asked.

"No, I was blindfolded the entire time and he rarely spoke."

"Do you have any idea of just where you were?"

"No, he must have drugged me in the laboratory that night, and when I awoke, I was bound to a chair and blindfolded. After that, he kept me isolated in a dark room."

Her wrists and ankles were bruised which attested her brutal imprisonment.

Monti mused, "Seems we are no closer to capturing this devil. We must inform the judge and decide where we go from here. The killer certainly has maintained the edge on us."

Seven

The judge was appalled when learning of last night's events.

"I was attending the village board meeting in the Park when the lights went dark. We thought the generator malfunctioned and by the time we rounded up the plant operator in town I guess the drama had long ended" commented the judge. He questioned,

"Why didn't you inform me of all this before now?"

Attempting to be diplomatic, Monti explained,

"Your honor, we didn't think it wise at the time to enlist and possibly endanger others. We didn't even notify Dillon."

"Just as well with him, he's been laid-up with an injury. He fell from his horse and sprained his leg. Rumor has it that, as usual, he was inebriated when leaving the pub in town. The big question now is, how do we proceed?"

Carrie's father piped in, "I suggest we contact the state police and even organize a state militia."

The judge emphatically interjected: "The residents of the Park are maddeningly jealous of their privacy and even worse with their reputations. Why, that's all the city gossip columnists need to hear and we'd see a total exodus from the Park with property value's nose diving."

"I suggest we continue to enlist our newly formed deputy squad. We'll need to finance a large construction project in the Park, say, rebuilding the dam which it needs anyway, to use as a cover for all of the non-Park people that will be roaming about. And we could hire one or two to bartend in the club. This way we will have an added measure of security. Carrie and I will continue to move about with our eyes open."

"Monti, I agree. I can't think of anything else we could do at this time. We need to casually continue with our lives as before. Let's hold a meeting with the constable and village mayor. Although we'll need to have the mayor's vow of secrecy."

"I object!" Exclaimed Samuels as he jumped from his chair. "I simply cannot condone the continued exposure of my daughter to this fiend any longer! Hasn't she suffered enough? Carrie, you will return with me to the city immediately!"

Carrie couldn't dream of leaving Monti at this time, or at any time, ever. She emotionally responded: "Father, I will not leave the Park. I too have a score to settle with this monster and I'm staying here!" Samuels had already detected a magnetic attraction between his daughter and Monti, surmising a serious relationship had developed between the two.

"Then if you're determined to stay, I will also. We can rent a suite at the club. After all, I also have a score to settle with this murderous scoundrel!"

* * *

The next morning the judge called a meeting with the village mayor, Tom Haggerty. Haggerty was the quintessential politician, a fast talking, ingratiating windbag. His longevity in office was based solely on the secrets he held of many of the Park's leading citizens: peccadillos with others' wives, any of their past criminal records, et cetera. He was appalled upon learning of the recent events but primarily concerned with maintaining the Park's reputation.

"Certainly we will hire the deputies. And be assured, I will keep silent with the board members regarding their undercover assignments. However, I will expect progress on the dam refurbishment, this will be a considerable investment. Constable Dillon, will you vouch for the honesty and integrity of the men selected?"

"I definitely will vouch for them mayor and we can totally count on their keeping the mission to themselves."

The judge also suggested to the mayor that a crew should be hired and assigned to walk the roadways surveying and inspecting the many utility poles and their electric lamps. "This will provide good cover for both a roving daylight and nighttime security team" observed the judge.

Monti chimed in, "They all must report to us anything they see that's unusual or out of the ordinary. Any new faces that appear in the Park even any gossip they may pick up."

"Monti, I want you to be the coordinator in this. Constable, you will inform him with anything you learn from the men. And instruct them to not, I say again, not take anything into their own hands; everything must go through Doctor Montigue-Smith."

"Yes judge, I will advise the men and keep the doctor informed."

Work began on the dam immediately along with the roadway security. The dam project required a draw-down on the lake enabling the spalling concrete surface to be refaced and a new spillway had to be introduced. The preliminary work of site surveying, excavation and materials delivery continued into the spring providing a good cover for the dozen or so men that would last throughout the summer. A two-man team continuously patrolled the roads with a horse and wagon. The judge convinced the club's president that the quality of service in the bar and also the domestic staff had degraded and a staff augmentation was required, so three undercover deputies were assigned to the club. With all these details in place, the group of man hunters settled down into normal Park life as they surveilled.

J.T.

The following weeks were quiet and routine. Although subtle changes had taken hold with some people. Monti and Carrie returned to their travels to Sing Sing, however for only two or three days a week. Samuels became a familiar face at the club and, despite his modest social position, was accepted as an equal at the endless rounds of dinner parties and golf outings. The judge began packing a gun, a habit he left behind since the rebel war. Even Dillon seemed to quell his drinking habit by spending less time at the pub in town.

Monti and Carrie's relationship intensified in both their scientific collaboration and personal feelings. Her book manuscript began to bulge with numerous case studies but in a disjointed array of observations, footnotes and references. Monti assumed the role of editor.

"Carrie my dear, you have assembled much important data, however, I think it's now time to summarize and present your thesis. In fact, our dreadful experiences here in the Park could be a very good vehicle."

"You are right my love, but you and I haven't reconciled our different theories on motivation. I still think the prime factor is environmental."

"Alright, let's discuss this in the context of the incidents here in the Park, which, are similar to the stories of the Sing Sing mass murderers. First, they all are very cunning which they must be, otherwise they would be caught after the first murder. They have the intelligence to carefully pick their targets, plan their escape routes and filter into regular society.

"They have enough time on their hands to plan their evil deeds and then to execute them. This is not indicative of a poor upbringing. This means they do have time available, something that a lower class person working sixty hours a week doesn't. So they have personal resources which many, not enjoying inheritance, or education or talent, lack. And lastly, from the many brains I've dissected, both of normal and abnormal people, I've found in many of the abnormal, a distinct difference in the tissue structure.

"Therefore, I believe although their home life, say if it's tumultuous may have a bearing, it's not the entire picture. In fact, I think it may be much less influential than a biological cause. An event may occur that triggers their heinous actions. Once they savor their evil deed, they cannot stop."

Carrie countered, "So you don't believe poverty, a one parent household, or abuse, or alcoholism can be the cause? Where these conditions develop a deep hatred and distrust in the individual causing him to strike back?"

"Perhaps a contributor, but not the total cause. Many are raised under those conditions and do not commit mass murder. If it were so, the majority of society would be out killing people."

"Well, I'm still not convinced."

After quietly pondering these issues for a few minutes, she asked,

"Maybe I should consider exploring both of these issues in the book? Since there is no conclusive proof either way."

"Ah, an excellent thought! I'll work with you on that if you wish?" With that agreement they began to finalize Carrie's book.

***

As in the past, conditions in the Park seemed to settle into a permanent normalcy. Monti observed how quickly people seem to adopt their regular ways once a threat recedes. Over the summer the dam repairs were completed. The horrors of the past seemed to have ended so the judge advised the constable to release the deputies. Carrie's father had already returned to the demands of his business in the city.

"Monti darling, do you think the murderous rampage has finally ended?"

"I don't know. The pattern of the past was a period of mayhem followed by a lull. When complacency set in, the madman would strike again. However, it's human nature to drop ones guard when all seems well. I just don't know dear. People simply can't live in terror forever. My concern though, is once all becomes quiet and content, he will strike again."

"Maybe he has left the area or even died! Remember the terror in London years ago with the Ripper murders? He struck numerous times then abruptly stopped."

"Yes Carrie, I remember that well. My uncle Simon worked in London at the time. He would reminisce of the grave terror during that period; people were fearful to be on the streets of White Chapel after dark. Many wouldn't even venture out in the safer sections of London. And that is the puzzle, he just stopped and was never found, a mystery never solved."

Following the publication of her book, which was the ticket for Carrie completing her medical degree, she and Monti decided to marry.

eight

A full year had elapsed since the murderer had abducted Carrie. The Park residents and even the judge confidently concluded the danger was buried within the soon to be forgotten history of the Park.

J.T.

A small, exclusive wedding was held in New York City with the bride and groom immediately boarding a steamship for an extended European Honeymoon. Jones was to stay in the Park and tend to the mansion. Their plan was for a six month, grand tour of the continent with a first stop and brief stay at the estate of Monti's uncle in England.

Uncle Simon was a member of the British landed gentry and the House of Lords. He lived in a modest country estate of fifty rooms, centered on three thousand acres in the Cotswold's. An octogenarian with a white walrus mustache and a full head of white hair, parted in the middle that hung out over his ears appearing like the spread wings of a Canada goose gliding to a landing.

"Ah my boy it is good to see you and your gorgeous young bride! My word, but she is very gorgeous!"

"Uncle Simon, it is good to see you also! This is Carrie."

"Hello Uncle Simon." Said Carrie as she attempted a modified curtsy.

As they sat in the drawing room, Carrie was amazed at the size and opulence of the surroundings. The huge room was paneled in lacquered oak, covered all about with the mounted heads of animals from three continents. At one end of the room, a fireplace of walk-in size contained a stack of crackling logs; a huge Bengal Tiger rug was sprawled across the parquet floor.

"Well my boy, tell us about your little Tuxedo Park. We've hosted some of your neighbors here during their travels. A strange lot those Americans."

"Uncle Simon, we've had a terrible time recently. A madman was stalking about causing mayhem that even threatened Carrie. And, unfortunately, he's still at large."

Monti continued to explain the gory details.

"My word, if it doesn't sound like Jack the Ripper all over again. You know we had a bloody awful time with that demon back in the 80s."

"Yes, I know. In fact, we'd like to hear more about that. As you know, Carrie and I have a deep interest in that type of criminal."

"Well, you and your little lady must first settle in. We will have plenty of time for discussing that. You both need to freshen-up from your long journey."

At that, Monti and Carrie retired for the afternoon.

After a sumptuous dinner, they again retired to the drawing room, Monti with his pipe and Uncle Simon with his brandy and cigar. Carrie, tired from the many days of travel excused herself early.

"That's a fine young lady you've got there Monti."

"Yes uncle, I know. And she's as smart as she is pretty. I'm very lucky."

Over the next two weeks, Monti and Carrie immersed themselves into the manor's grand lifestyle. Afternoon luncheons with members of the aristocracy were the norm as was morning shooting or fox hunting. Their first attempt on riding to the hounds became a minor adventure for Carrie. Being unprepared as she was not an avid or experienced horsewoman, Carrie borrowed a riding outfit from one of the hunting regulars. Being the courageous sport, she attempted to participate.

"But Monti darling, as a city girl, I'm really only a novice rider. The extent of my experience has been on maintained roads, not cross country. I've never jumped a fence or even ridden in the forest."

"Oh my dear, not to worry. We'll take it slow, drop behind and go on our own way. It would be rude to simply decline their hospitality and besides, we may meet some interesting people."

On the morning of the hunt the sun shone beautifully as the troop of riders assembled. However, the horse assigned to Carrie was a bit too spirited for her skill level and she created a bit of a ruckus while struggling to control the animal. As the horse began to buck and neigh, Uncle Simon called out:

"Monti and Carrie, I wish to introduce an old friend, Arthur Conan Doyle."

"My word Carrie, we must meet him!"

Monti cantered over with Carrie trailing behind. As Monti opened with his greeting:

"Sir, it's a great pleasure to meet you." Carrie's horse bolted taking them both at breakneck speed from the paddock, through the stone archway and across the lawn. Heads turned and Monti went off in pursuit. Over the rolling hills they rode as Carrie grasped the spooked horse's neck for dear life. Finally, as the horse's stamina was blown out, they came to a halt as Monti rode up.

"Well that was a fine introduction to the great Arthur Conan Doyle dear! You may even have earned a place in his next Sherlock Holmes tale with that great show of derring-do. Or perhaps Buffalo Bill could place you on the payroll."

"Don't be funny Monti, I told you I'm not well suited for this. I've never been so embarrassed. What must they think of me!"

"Oh dear, don't be concerned, on occasion everyone encounters a rambunctious horse. At least you remained in the saddle, although somewhat inelegantly."

To preclude a reoccurrence of the adventure, Carrie rode back to the stables behind Monti on his horse, with her horse trailing behind.

* * *

At dinner that evening Uncle Simon seated Monti and Carrie next to Conan Doyle. Doyle was trained as a medical doctor, but rather than medicine, he gained fame for his mystery stories, namely those featuring the great sleuth, Sherlock Holmes. He and Simon became fast friends years ago when Conan Doyle was a student and Simon was lecturing at the University of Edinburgh.

Upon meeting the famous author, Monti once again extended his hand with a fresh reintroduction. "Once again Sir, my name is Monti and this is Carrie."

"My word, you and the lady certainly had an exhilarating ride. As such, you didn't miss a thing with the fox hunt, it was a total bust."

"Sir, I apologize for our abrupt departure."

"Rubbish. You gave us all a great laugh." With that comment, Carrie flushed a cherry red.

"Mr. Doyle."

"Oh, please just call me Conan."

"Well Conan, We have greatly enjoyed your Sherlock Holmes series. They indicate a very deep insight into the criminal mind which I speculate is the result of your medical training. Both Carrie and I have similar interests, so perhaps we could spend some time together and commiserate on this?"

"Certainly young man, I would love to."

After dinner the three retired to the drawing room. Although fifteen years his junior, Carrie was immediately captivated by Doyle. The tall, stout, Doyle wore a glorious handlebar mustache and spoke in the King's English with a slight Scottish brogue, and he was immensely intelligent.

"I really didn't fare well in medicine. In fact, at one time, my resources were diminished down to two pounds. As I whiled away the hours in my office in Scotland, waiting for a patient to emerge, I began scribbling short stories. As time passed, I began to pick up a few shillings here and there from writing in the periodicals and completely abandoned medicine altogether in preference for writing."

"In doing so Sir, you invented a totally new way of investigating crime that is by detailed analysis. This is a technique which I also apply."

"Well, you know I am not the originator of that process. I owe that concept to a man who was a great friend of your uncle, his name was Doctor Joseph Bell whom I studied under. Yes, good old Bell was a genius in the art of diagnosis. When a new patient arrived with an ailment, Bell could, more often than not, arrive at the problem even before the patient spoke."

"And how did he do that?" a startled Carrie questioned.

"He would immediately scrutinize the patient's gait, his manner of speech, the pallor of his skin, his style of clothing while gauging these and other features he would instantly draw conclusions. He was a master at combining various clues that most would not even consider. So in my writing, I applied these qualities to Mr. Sherlock Holmes."

"As both an engineer and medical practitioner, I too use these techniques."

"My friends, let's hope the future of what's now being called 'forensic science' becomes a widely used approach to crime solving. Some are even starting to consider the apparent uniqueness of skin dissimilarities in the fingertips as clues" commented Conan Doyle.

Monti and Carrie spent the remainder of the evening with the great storyteller describing the ghastly details of their experiences in the Park. He listened very attentively, occasionally offering various insights.

As the days wore on, the newlyweds became increasingly restless at the manor house and started to become somewhat self-conscious by presenting the appearance they were overusing Uncle Simon's hospitality. Just as they were beginning to plan the next trip on their honeymoon odyssey, a telegram arrived for Doctor Montague-Smith.

"My word Carrie, would you believe it! I'm being inducted into the Royal Geographic Society!"

"Oh my dear, what an honor, but for what?"

"The telegram states only: 'For your groundbreaking work with the ethnographic analysis of the Zulu Nation of Southern Africa in the years 1893 and 1894.' This must have resulted from the paper I presented two years ago at the Conference on 'The Indigenous Peoples of Sub-Saharan Africa.'"

"We must immediately journey to London. The next meeting of the society's board of governors is in three days."

The next morning, after hastily packing their bags and bidding Uncle Simon farewell they boarded the morning train to the big city. A meeting with the great Sir Clements Robert Markham, president of the society was in order before being presented to the governors. Markham, besides being well known for his huge mutton chop sideburns, had been on the search in the artic for the lost expedition of Sir John Franklin and he worked under Sir Robert Napier as his geographer before accepting the society's presidency.

The Royal Geographic Society was the most famous exploratory organization in the world. Founded in 1830, its many luminaries included Charles Darwin, David Livingston, Henry Morton Stanley and many of the other great scientists and explorers of the 19th Century.

"Ah, Doctor Montague-Smith, it is good to meet you. And I presume this is the Mrs.?" Questioned Markham.

"Yes and no" responded Monti. "This is also *Doctor* Montague-Smith and also the Mrs. Montague-Smith." With a tinge of embarrassment, Markham extended his hand to Carrie asking, "Are you a medical doctor also my dear?"

"Yes I am and the Doctor and I are both colleagues in the same endeavor."

"Excellent!" Exclaimed Markham.

"Your common endeavor is something I wish to discuss. As you know, you have been nominated for the position of Fellow of the Royal Geographic Society. This distinction is being bestowed based on the fine work you accomplished with the Zulus a few years ago. We now wish to make you an offer to continue that work under the auspices of the society."

"What? Well, this is totally unexpected! We are interested in the inner workings of the human mind as it relates to violence, not African tribal life. Your proposal is both unexpected and far afield of our interests" responded Monti.

"Oh doctors, that is not necessarily so. We are interested in sponsoring a nine month sabbatical for you, and now probably for your wife also, to investigate and record the habits, customs and social interplay of some of the indigenous tribes of Central Africa. As you know, these qualities are developed not only by environmental influence, but also emerge from deep within the psyche. And if the workings of the mind are your interest, well, you'll have multiple societies to probe."

"Sir Markham, the society is offering a very interesting and generous proposal. However, it is a very sudden and perhaps a far departure from our former plans. Before we're prepared to make a decision, my wife Carrie and I must think about this."

"Oh of course, but I must prepare you, the board of governors will raise this issue."

Leaving the society's building, Carrie challenged Monti,

"Darling, this could be a wonderful opportunity. Think of the vast reservoir of humanity, many unstudied peoples that we would have access to. It would be an incredible experience and the opportunity to break new ground!"

"Yes dear, it would. But first, living in the bush is very harsh and dangerous. Many of these people are warlike and not civilized in our understanding of the word. I'm not sure I want to expose you to that. And it's not where we want to focus our investigations."

"Oh but yes it is. Is violence peculiar to only the white, civilized races? Do we have civilized motives for killing each other while they may not? What are their motives? I think this is very pertinent to our studies. And regarding my being exposed to danger, Africa can't be any more dangerous for me than being among the 'civilized' in Tuxedo Park has been!"

"Carrie my dear, you pose very strong arguments, but I'm still very apprehensive."

"Darling, perhaps your accepting this assignment was a consideration when they agreed to your induction into the Royal Geographic Society."

"You mean a quid pro quo?"

"Well, I don't know. But what we do know is that they think very highly of you and are willing to invest in your ability."

✳ ✳ ✳

"Members of the board, I'm very pleased to introduce Doctors Montigue-Smith, both who are eminent practitioners of the science of the mind."

"Gentlemen of the board, my wife and I are much honored to be here today and being presented to this august group."

Following Monti's introduction, Markham wasted no time in conducting the ceremony:

"Members of the board of governors of the Royal Geographic Society due hereby appoint, Doctor James Isambard Kingdom Brunel Montigue-Smith, with the support and agreement of his Royal Majesty, the King, and for his outstanding work in the realm of human understanding and for his groundbreaking work with the ethnographic analysis of the Zulu Nation of Southern Africa in the years 1893 and 1894, the position of Fellow of the Royal Geographic Society.

"Do I have a second?"

"I'll second." Spoke Quincy St. John Throckmorton.

"All those in favor vote aye, those opposed, nay."

The entire board immediately voted in favor and Monti was then sworn in.

Markham then addressed the board, "gentlemen, I have briefly discussed with the doctors our proposal regarding an ethnographic study of other indigenous tribes of Africa. As you all know, many of these primitive people, despite our long history of exploration on the Dark Continent, are still a basically unknown entity. Enquires of the distinguished doctors could open an enormous trove of knowledge and understanding in that regard."

One of the board members then spoke up and addressed Monti:

"Doctor Montigue-Smith, what is your opinion on this proposal?"

Monti and Carrie spent much of the previous night discussing the issue and Carrie's strong argument eventually won over Monti's apprehensions.

"Sir, my wife and I considered the society's generous proposal at length and decided to accept."

"Jolly good show!" Exclaimed the board member as the others nodded in enthusiastic agreement.

"However," Monti continued, "we feel strongly that the greatest benefit to our understanding of these people, and I must say, that which will be the most challenging will be the study of the more war-like tribes. So, we decided on selecting two of the most belligerent, the Maasai people and the Wa-Kikuyu. Who incidentally, are traditional enemies as they are of a totally different ethnicity; the Maasi being a Nilotic group with the Kikuyu being Bantu."

"Doctor, in that regard, you are the expert" commented Markham.

Monti was charged with studying the cultural and ethnographic differences of different African tribes. His personal curiosity and interest was whether there was any evidence of cold blooded murder particularly mass killings occurring in any of these cultures, i.e. violence without any rational need for the tribes' existence.

Since he was intimately knowledgeable about the Zulu's, having lived with them, he would focus on the Maasi and Wa-Kikuyu, two prominent, but ethnologically different peoples living further north in central Africa.

* * *

So now the big push for Monti and Carrie was to assemble their kit and book passage to Mombasa. They traipsed about London assembling safari clothing, tents, and camp equipment, food stuff, et cetera. Although Monti had taken his Mannlicher, its modest caliber was simply inadequate for Africa's dangerous game, so he spent an afternoon at the Holland & Holland establishment and purchased a . 475 magnum, double rifle.

Before departing London, Monti exchanged his biweekly telegram with Jones. He established this policy to keep track of activities within the Park during their absence in Europe. Fortunately until now, all had been quite in the Park. His message to Jones read:

-Jones anything new in park STOP we are sailing for Africa STOP we will be there 6-9 months STOP will post details from there-

nine

Many years later, Doctor Montigue-Smith provided me the following details of their adventures in Africa during my three night stay at the mansion, which I will now recount for the readers. This diversion for the newlyweds unfortunately ushered in a new wave of mayhem within the Park. During their absence, a series of dastardly occurrences began, once again.

J.T.

The outward-bound trip aboard a 19th Century steamship was a long and arduous voyage. The circuitous journey tracked the European coast past Gibraltar, on into the Mediterranean, crossing its full length then through the Suez Canal and then down the Red Sea, around the Horn of Africa and then down the east coast to the ancient port city of Mombasa—in stifling heat for much of the trip.

On arrival, the first stop was the office of Sir. William Montrose, the representative for British East Africa.

"My heavens Doctor, you two will be living with the Massai and Wa-Kikuyu? These two are some of the most warlike tribes in all of Africa! Even the British Army avoids noodling with those beggars. They go around rather than trespass Massi territory. And the Kikuyu now have a white chieftain who's a bit of a loony Yorkshireman, claiming to be their king. You'll be embarking on a very dicey journey!"

"Sir, I've already spent considerable time living with the Zulu's."

"Yes, but their warlike habits were subdued back in the 80s." responded Montrose.

"Well, you are right there, but we must continue on anyway. Can you recommend a trustworthy guide?"

"I jolly well can. A chap named Kijana Mdogo. That's his name in Swahili, in English his name means 'small boy.' We just call him Kijana. He' a capital fellow, honest, courageous and loyal. I'll send him to your hotel. If you are determined to carry on, you have my best of luck."

While sitting on the hotel veranda after dinner, Monti commented,

"I hope we're doing the right thing with you being here my love."

"Yes darling, we are. From this experience we'll discover new information regarding these people, acquire more than enough material for a book and have an exciting time as a result."

Just as she finished speaking a table boy informed them that someone wished to speak with them outside.

Standing at the bottom of the veranda's steps was a young, thinly built native wearing a tarboosh with a blanket slung over his shoulder. His forearms were wrapped in copper wire and he had slit earlobes containing a spent cartridge shell in each.

"Jambo Bwana! My name is Kijana Mdogo. Bwana Montrose sent me."

"Well Jambo Kijana Mdogo, my name is Bwana Monti, and this is my wife, Carrie."

"Bwana, no understand, wefe Carrie."

"No, it's wife."

"Wefe."

"No, oh, how do you say madam."

"Ah . . . ah maaa dam, yes, Swahili mean, mwanamke."

"My word Kijana, I can't even pronounce that! How do you say doctor in Swahili?"

"Ah, dac tor, Swahili mean daktari."

"Very well then . . . it's Daktari Carrie."

They spent the next two mornings in the market hiring native porters.

"Kijana, how many porters will be required?"

"Twenty-two, Bwana."

"Why twenty-two?"

"Twenty to carry load and two to return horses."

"Return the horses, from where?"

"We go Kikuyu Land first. Maybe two days on train flatcar, porters and horses. Then three days on horses, then two porters return horses, and then we walk three days in bush with twenty porters."

Carrie questioned, "Why walk when we have horses?"

"Must walk, too many buzz, buzz" Kijana commented as he shook his hands in front of his face.

"Darling, he means we will be traveling across land where the Tsetse fly exists. They are deadly for any livestock."

"Deadly for livestock! What about humans?"

"Yes, they have been known to carry the sleeping sickness, but we must take the chance if we expect to travel upcountry. Hopefully we'll only have to suffer the stings."

After renting the horses and loading the flatcar with porters, supplies and their mounts, they boarded the Uganda railway which was euphemistically called the 'Lunatic Line' by the settlers for its cost in men and British pounds. The line was not yet completed, having been halted in the mountains by two man-eating lions that were decimating the track gang at Tsavo. But it would take them far enough on their journey.

In Meru, they left the train and began their journey on horseback as the line of porters trailed behind. Kijana continually policed the line to keep it moving along as Monti and Carrie rode at the front. Each porter carried sixty pounds of equipment and supplies through the stifling heat while they sang a monotonous dirge, accompanied by the beating of a drum. The line of march would occasionally be halted as Monti shot an antelope or two to feed the large contingent of men. A hastily built camp was erected each night with Kijana preparing a meal consumed around a large campfire.

Despite the difficulty of horseback riding over very broken ground, Monti was more worried about Carrie's ability to continue on foot once the horses were released.

"Carrie my dear, how are you holding up?"

"Well enough, I guess. I will be happy however, when we arrive at our final destination. I wonder how Tuxedo Park is faring."

"Yes, I wonder too. Our communications now will be limited to an occasional letter delivered by runner. That will be an extended delay."

* * *

After their trip through the highlands, they emerged from the forested hills onto the vast open veld of central British East Africa. From here on the trip was on foot. They now viewed enormous herds of wildebeest and zebra, various antelope, packs of wild dog and roving prides of lion. They marveled at the wide diversity of animals from the peculiar necks of the giraffe and gerenuk to the tall, sleek bodies of the cheetah. Their human column would occasionally be halted and sometimes waylaid when encountering a belligerent rhinoceros or string of elephants.

On the morning of the second day of their foot journey, they were shocked to see that their entire native porter staff had abandoned them and absconded with much of their food.

"My word Kijana, where have they all gone!?" Exclaimed Monti.

"I think Bwana, they too scarred, they leave. We too close to Kikuyu."

"Well this is a fine fix we're in! How far do we have to go, Kijana?" Questioned Carrie.

"Maybe one day, Doctari, maybe two. We know soon, Kikuyu find us."

"Need we be worried about them?"

"Maybe . . . yes, Doctari."

The three sorted through the remaining supplies and gathered together some clothing, ammunition, their medical kit, blankets, compass, and writing materials. They then continued their trek across the savanna.

As the sun was setting they decided to camp near a water hole. Monti questioned, "Kijana, I'd like to build a fire to keep the animals at bay, however, I don't wish to announce ourselves to the Kikiyu prematurely. What do you think?"

"No matter Bawana, they find us soon."

"Do you think they'll be hostile?"

"Kijana not know. Some say Kikyu have white chief now, and you two white."

"Dear, this may be a good thing. Certainly if a white man is leading them, they will be friendly."

"I don't know Carrie. Who knows, if a white man is actually their chief, and if so, what his intentions may be?"

"Well, maybe he's as you were with the Zulus—studying them. And if he is, that will be a big asset to our investigations."

"Let's hope the white man, if in fact there is one living with them has good intensions."

Early the next morning, Kijana hurriedly awoke Monti and gestured in a circular motion. As he raised his head, he viewed, standing above them, and totally encircling the rise around the waterhole, dozens of native warriors. They silently stood shoulder to shoulder, some wearing high headdresses made from lion's manes; others had their entire faces encircled by a furry ring made of the black fur of the colobus monkey. All had their faces and bodies colored with white paint; they held long spears and carried multi-colored, buffalo hide shields.

Monti gently nudged Carrie awake. She gasped when opening her eyes as she gazed upon the wild, intimidating spectacle above. The warriors remained silent for an interminable period of time and then an opening appeared in the ring of natives as Monti and Carrie remained transfixed.

A tall intimidating form walked toward them, arrayed similar to the warriors but with a leopard skin across his shoulder.

The warrior leader addressed Kijana:

"nini wewe kuja hapa?"

"Kijana, do you understand him?" Monti questioned.

"Yes Bwana, he speak Swahili. He ask why do we come here."

"Tell him we wish to meet his chief."

"tunataka kukutana mkuu yako"

The warrior responded: "kufuata"

"He say follow, Bwana."

The leader then motioned to the throng above and pointed to the provisions lying on the ground. Three warriors descended into the camp and secured all of their belongings including their guns.

The ominous demand to follow initiated a long single-file, four-hour hike across the savanna with Monti, Carrie and Kijana sequestered in the center of the column as prisoners. In the mid-day heat, Carrie was barely able to keep pace with warriors whose gait and incredible stamina even taxed Monti and Kijana. However, she had no choice but to stumble along.

By mid-afternoon they arrived, somewhat frazzled at a huge kraal centered in the basin of a large valley which Monti surmised was the caldera of an extinct volcano. The village was encircled by a large stockade constructed of ten foot high vertical logs, sharpened to points, similar to the defensive wall used in colonial American times for frontier fortresses. Within this enclosure grazed stray cattle with dogs and children running about. The three were led to a hut where they were directed to stay. To insure their containment, an imposing warrior was placed at the entrance to stand guard.

"Well this doesn't look very good" commented Carrie.

"Doctari, this very good. They no kill us . . . yet."

"He's right Carrie. The Kikuyu are said to not tolerate anyone trespassing in their territory, particularly white men. So, there is a reason why we weren't immediately killed."

Shortly thereafter, a young girl entered the hut carrying gourds of water and food.

"What is this?" Carrie commented when inspecting the pasty appearing mush.

"It is a type of gruel concocted of maize and goats milk. A very common food staple in many regions of Africa" responded Monti.

After a while, a contingent of warriors entered the hut motioning the captives to follow. They were led through a large, chanting crowd to the center of the village. As they walked through the thronging mass, loud drums were sounding a fast, thumping beat as the women cried out intermittent wails and clucking sounds. Some shook rattles to the beat as others stomped their feet in unison which sounded bells on their ankles. The cacophony of noise was frightening as well as earsplitting to the trio.

At the center of the mob, elevated on a crudely constructed chair of split logs sat an astounding figure. He wore a tall lion mane headdress, his face and bare chest painted white with diagonal black and red stripes on his face with small circles in black across his shoulders. His midriff and legs were covered with a leopard skin cloak. His right hand clutched a carved walking stick with a handle made of a warthog tusk. The wrists were ringed with numerous brass wire bracelets.

As he raised his hand the clamorous noise immediately stopped.

"nini wewe kuja nchi ya Kikuyu?" he questioned.

"What did he say Kijana?"

"He ask 'Why do you come to the land of the Kikuyu' Bwana."

"Tell him we come in peace and wish to learn about the Kikuyu."

"Mwambie sisi kuja kwa amani na unataka kujifunza kuhusu Kikuyu."

The chief then directly addressed the two white intruders in perfect Queens English: "So you wish to learn about the Kikuyu? Why?"

Both Monti and Carrie were so astounded, they were momentarily struck mute. Gaining their composure, Monti replied,

"My name is Monti and this is Carrie, we're scientists and wish to study the Kikuyu culture. And my word, how did you learn to speak English?"

"Are any other whites coming behind you?"

"Why no, we're alone" responded Monti.

"You two are very courageous and very stupid for trespassing in Kikuyuland. Outsiders, who do trespass, never leave here alive. I am King of the Kikuyu."

With a wave of his hand he dismissed the three and they were taken back to their makeshift jail.

From here I must digress for the moment and inform the reader of the events that took place during Monti and Carrie's absence. The strange and unexplainable occurrences of the past, once again began anew:

The elderly schoolmarm, Gladys Ross was found opposite the train tracks near the station in town; she was decapitated. Some considered this to be either a suicide or dreadful accident. The Park murders of the past were discounted as this tragedy occurred outside the Park gate, and besides, the Park had been very quiet for many months. The only doubtful voice was that of the new county sheriff, Tom Watson.

Constable Dillon had retired complaining of pain and disability resulting from falling from his horse last year. However, most considered this just an excuse, the real ailment being his ongoing addiction to drink.

Watson's skepticism centered on the boot prints found near the body. Prints of a large size produced by riding boots, certainly not worn by the schoolmarm.

J.T.

ten

Monti and Carrie, along with Kijana were once again summoned from their hut and brought to a large circular structure. The building was constructed of tightly woven thatch. The inside was decorated with numerous wall hangings of zebra, cheetah, and giraffe hides. At the center of the enclosure was a large log-burning fire, the smoke exiting through a circular opening in the roof. At the far end sat the Kikuyu King on his wooden throne, two huge elephant tusks forming an arch over his head. The lion headdress was removed exposing long red, braided locks lying across his shoulders.

"Please enter and sit down. My Christian name is John Boyes; the natives call me Mfalme Umbopo. That is, King Umbopo."

"Good grief, Mr. Boyes!" Exclaimed Monti.

"Please call me John."

"How on earth did you become King of these blackguards?"

"Well, it's quite a long story you see. I'm originally from Yorkshire. After a few years knocking about as a seaman, I landed at Durban in Cape Colony. I then trekked north to Bulawayo, and entered service in the Afrikander Corp. and fought in the Matebele War. When that ended I decided to trek upcountry and try my hand at trading. I entered this country two years ago as a trader supplying the track gang coolies building the Uganda Railroad. I needed foodstuffs and this country is rich in maize and wild game. So I arrived here expecting to garner all that I would need."

"What a story! How on earth did you pacify the natives?"

"Actually, somewhat by guile and much luck although they're not at all yet pacified. I happened to enter

Kikuyuland when two of the Kikuyu clans were at war. One attempted to attack my column, and, as they had never been exposed to guns before, my rifle fire scared them off. And later as they tracked us and saw my red hair and white skin, well, they assumed I was a spirit.

"I then realized if I were to have any success in this country, I needed to gain their support and end their disruptive warring. Through much parleying, and with a little bit of the white man's magic, I not only gained their confidence ending their inter-clan warfare, but over time they made me their King! So now I've maintained a prosperous trading business, but I also try to civilize the clans as best I can. But they have a long way to go."

"We've heard about you in Mombasa, but to most, you are a rumor bordering on myth."

"Yes, the authorities are very unhappy with my position here. They only tolerate me for the needs of the railway construction. So, they keep my existence somewhere between fact and fiction. When the construction ends, they will no doubt attempt to shut me down and pacify the natives. You know this land is very fertile and they'd love to see it populated by white settlers."

"That will certainly be a challenge" Monti commented.

"Yes, I fear much bloodshed will occur before that happens. Now just what do you two expect to do here?"

Carrie chimed in, "Monti and I are both medical doctors. We're here at the request of the Royal Geographic Society to study the warlike tribes of both the Kikuyu and Maasi."

"That's quite a tall order. As you know, these people do not welcome strangers. In fact, if I had not interceded, the three of you would have been killed long before now."

"Yes, and we certainly are indebted!"

"Just what do you expect to study here?"

Monti responded, "Actually, we're in good luck, not only for having met you, but having access to two of the most violent tribes in Africa. Their propensity for war making is just what we're interested in. Our interest is to determine what motivates the killing of one person by another beyond the obvious motivations of anger, personal gain and so forth. Particularly those individuals who continue to randomly kill numerous times for no particular reason."

"When it comes to killing, this is certainly ripe territory. But the motivations are a set of issues you'll need to discover on your own. Although the Kikuyu are adamant regarding any other white men within their territory, I can make them accept you. I will hold a shauri, which is their version of a council and inform them you bring big medicine and they need to honor you. They all harbor many ailments living as they do, so you'll need to tend to them for their needs. This will elevate you in their eyes."

"Very well, we have brought some medical supplies." responded Carrie.

"Oh, one other favor if we may, how can we send a letter to our home?" questioned Monti.

"Write what you wish and I'll send a runner to Naivasha where it can be posted."

Hello my good man Jones,

Carrie and I have arrived in Africa and have the most extraordinary set of stories to relate to you upon our return, and I'm sure many more will develop in the coming days and weeks. And how are things going in Tuxedo Park? We received your last letter at the London address and all was well. I trust conditions are still suitably stable? When you write to us, address to: Captain Gorges, Naivasha Station, East African Protectorate.

Sincerely,
Monti
Post script- Send also the following medical supplies: quinine, idoform, isopropyl alcohol and bandages of various sizes.

King Umbopo had a large nyumba (or house) built for Monti and Carrie. Kijana had to make do with a small adjacent hut. To officially welcome the trio into the village, the King organized a shauri with all of the lesser chiefs and elders. Following this introduction, a large bullock was slaughtered and roasted over a huge fire. Having been amazed when first glimpsing John Boyes' red hair, the natives were totally enthralled with Carries long, fire-red locks. Many believed both Carrie and Boyes were sibling spirits, with Monti and Kijana being her slaves. So their acceptance by the tribe was absolute.

During the shauri, a cluster of chief hierarchy sat at one end of a large circle of natives with Monti and Carrie next to King Umbopo in the place of honor. Due to Carrie's perceived, exalted status, she was the constant object of curiosity and admiration by the savages. They would endlessly gather around to stroke her fiery hair and marvel at her pure white skin. After the meal, the natives held a dance which only the warriors participated in. Each would enter the ring of onlookers in succession, prancing and jumping with mock battle gestures as the surrounding crowd would stomp their feet in unison with the women wailing and clucking with enthusiastic support. The bells on their ankles and the stomping of feet being the only music. This martial display continued through much of the night.

As the days passed, and with the King's support, Monti and Carrie would spend mornings administering to the sick and injured of the village. As the natives were extremely superstitious, this further elevated their reputation as mystics in the eyes of the savages.

To conduct their scientific inquires, their afternoons were spent questioning the sub-chiefs and elders. This became a very difficult and disheartening exercise as neither Monti nor Carrie could speak the Kikuyu language. The conversations were translated from Swahili and then into English by Kijana, consequently much nuance and detail were lost. In frustration, they would spend evenings with Boyes to clarify the areas of confusion.

"So John," Monti would begin, "the warriors seem to have a very casual, matter of fact attitude about killing their fellow man. Their view of their enemy seems to be similar to the way we consider our opponents in a soccer match. Simply a routine challenge with no emotional concern for their fellow man."

"First off, you must realize that the native will tell you anything you wish to hear and usually it's all untrue. But I think you are seeing this in a far too superficial manner—that of a civilized white man, and be assured, there is no emotion involved. The attitudes of the Kikuyu and all the natives I have met are much more complex and practical. There is no sympathy or even empathy for each other. I think these sentiments exist only in more so called, developed cultures. The motivations here are a combination of either mysticism or basic need. Don't forget, basic survival here is much more difficult than in your culture. For example, each tribe or clan continuously war with their neighbors for cattle, or grazing rights, or arable land, and sometimes for slaves. A successful, burgeoning population continually needs additional resources. Their aversion to the white man entering their territory is basic survival. They know the whites are more powerful and will kill them and steal their land.

"When someone is wronged, he will go to a witchdoctor and have a spell imposed. Occasionally, jealously will motivate violence against another, for example if a chief or witchdoctor is being challenged by a competitor. Then one or the other will attempt to destroy the challenger. Consequently, no other emotions or derangements are involved.

"When they war they automatically kill all of their male enemies and take the women and children as slaves. This provides additional cheap labor and adds to the tribe's population. They don't even bury the dead warriors. They leave the corpses for the animals. In fact, as the warriors attack, they emit their war calls. The packs of hyena in the area will hear this and begin wailing in anticipation of the coming feast. I know of no other reason for the savage's violence. Your pursuit of individuals who kill others just for sport does not exist here from my experience."

"So, you know of no instances of an individual killing others without a practical motive?" Questioned Carrie.

"No, all of the violence has a practical motive. Your killer of random victims simply would not even enter their minds."

"So are we to assume the murderer in our town is the product of an advanced civilization?"

"I think that's for you doctors to figure out. Only on rare occasions a native will kill unreasonably. When it occurs, they ascribe it to mysticism, the placing of a hex. But I believe the reason, and mind you, it's very rare indeed, is when someone becomes sick from either eating or being mauled by a diseased animal. What you call rabies."

* * *

This unexpected realization did not deter Monti and Carrie from pursuing the possibility of murder being committed within the tribes by derangement. However, there were also many other peculiar and heretofore, unstudied rituals and customs for their analysis. After all, they did owe the geographic society a full report. They also anticipated what may be discovered with the Maasi.

eleven

Monti and Carrie continued their scientific studies and makeshift medical practice with the natives. And the continuous warfare certainly ensured a large stock of patients. Boyes spent considerable time away on either trading missions or raiding other villages. His motive, besides pursuing an adventurous life with the savages, was to earn his fortune trading with the natives for ivory.

The team of doctors maintained a steady stream of letter communications with Jones. The new technology of telegraphy and advances in the trans-Atlantic cable greatly reduced the time in sending messages back to the states. The longest segment in the link being with the runner to and from Naivasha. Consequently, they would wire to Tuxedo Park on a weekly basis, notwithstanding the two times the runners were killed, once by savages and the other time by a lion.

The package of medicines and a letter were one of the first communications received from Jones:

Dear Sir:

Greetings to you and the missus. I hope you both are well and safe. Enclosed are the medical supplies you requested. During your absence, much has occurred both in and out of the Park.

Our dear old Gladys Ross was found dead by the train tracks in town. Her death being under very suspicious circumstances. The mystery is a boot print found at the site of her death. The constable has retired both from his job and humanity, preferring to live in his cups. Judge Martin has used his influence in Goshen which has assigned a full-time sheriff to replace Dillon. Incidentally, Sheriff Watson thinks the boot prints are suspicious, as they are not the type or size which would be worn by Mrs. Ross. If you need any other supplies, I shall send them along.

Your devoted servant,
Jones

"Good Grief Carrie, you must read this!"

". . . Yes dear, this is very troubling. Do you think this is him again?" Responded Carrie after digesting the communiqué.

"Well, I don't know. I wish Jones was a little more explicit in describing the boot. I think I will immediately respond back. I hope this new sheriff is a capital fellow and investigates further."

"Yes, and didn't you say when that young lady was murdered you took a casting of the print?"

"Oh, I certainly did! I'll direct Jones to provide the sheriff with the imprint."

Monti and Carrie were unable to contain themselves during the two week round trip delay in communications. When Jones's note finally arrived, it read:

Dear Sir:

I provided Sheriff Watson with your boot casting of the Mills affair. Unfortunately, he was not as fastidious as you and neglected to take a casting of the boot tracks near Mrs. Ross's body. However, he said the marks were also made by a riding boot. He remembers the size looked larger than a size eleven, and by measurement, your boot casting is eleven and a half. He was very interested in learning all of the dreadful details of the past killings in the Park and your findings, all of which I explained.

Your devoted servant,
Jones

"Carrie my dear, I fear we may be reading just what I've dreaded all along."

"Monti, should we return?"

"No my sweet, we can't. We have a solemn commitment to the Royal Geographic Society and we must complete our studies. And besides, even a rushed trip back to the states will take many weeks. So we must continue here and hope for the best with the new sheriff."

During Monti and Carries extended stay in Africa, conditions in the Park worsened. Sheriff Watson continued his inquiries into the Park murders, generally, to no avail. As the weeks passed by and he studied the previous murders, he became more convinced that the death of Gladys Ross was no accident. I continued to work off and on at the manor house performing odd jobs under Jones's direction.

J.T.

One afternoon, a messenger came running into camp with a letter for Monti from the sheriff:

Dear Doctor Montigue-Smith,

My name is John Watson, and I've replaced Constable Dillon as the new sheriff for Tuxedo. I have been following-up on the past killings that you have been involved with here in the Park. A tragedy recently occurred in the death of a Mrs. Gladys Ross of which I am convinced was no accident. Now I have the sad obligation to inform you of another death that was definitely not an accident!

Colonel Henry Stafford McKinnon, a gentleman whom you may know, was found in his boathouse, bludgeoned to death with a polo mallet. After conducting considerable investigation and many interviews, I've narrowed down the possibilities to one suspect, Quincy Mortimer Thompson.

My suspicions are based upon two very significant pieces of evidence. One- Mr. Thompson is well known within sporting circles to be a very avid polo player, and Two- The boot print at the Ross murder scene was most assuredly produced by a riding boot. This print and yours taken from the Mills murder are similar in size to Thompson's. And incidentally, Thompson being a serious polo player, he frequently wears riding boots.

Considering your intimate knowledge of the past events, and your acquaintance with Mr. Thompson, I'd greatly appreciate your thoughts on this.

Your humble servant,
Sheriff, John Watson

"My word Carrie, the sheriff thinks Quincy Thompson may be the murderer!"

"Dear, you have said that he is a cad with a very questionable character."

"Yes my love, he is a lazy womanizer and an egocentric dullard, but murder . . . and on such a grand scale! No, I just can't believe it's Thompson. I will write back to the sheriff expressing my disagreement with his theory."

To the Honorable John Watson,

First, congratulations on your new assignment as sheriff for the Town of Tuxedo. I'm sure you will perform a splendid job. Regarding your suspicions of Mr. Thompson being implicated in the rash of killings in the Park, I totally disagree. I have in fact known Mr. Thompson for a considerable length of time. And although a somewhat disagreeable character, I cannot support the thought of him being a murderer. To your notion of evidence against Mr. Thompson, his boot size may be similar; however, have you checked the boot sizes of all of the men in Tuxedo Park? All who ride and wear boots? Regarding the polo mallet, many members of the Park play polo, and besides, someone from outside the Park may be a polo aficionado who wears riding boots.

I do not wish to deter you from your investigations, on the contrary, but wish to ensure all possibilities are covered by you rather than settle on one that may be near at hand.

Yours truly,
James I. Montague-Smith

This note from one of the most notable members of the community didn't sit well with the sheriff. He continued his pursuit of Thompson.

Although not moving any closer to understanding the vexing question of a random motivation for murder, Monti and Carrie concluded they had learned all they reasonably could regarding the Kikuyu culture. And having already spent over four months in Kikuyuland, they concluded it was time to move on. Before leaving, Boyes held a celebratory shauri in their honor. He also assigned the trio a guide named Ngomi, who spoke the Maasai language and a guard detail of ten warriors to accompany them to the Maasai territory.
J.T.

twelve

The land of the Maasai was farther south and west of the Kikuyu and much more open, being comprised mainly of rolling, seemingly endless savanna. Their land ranged from British East Africa to German East Africa in the south, past Mt. Kilimanjaro.

Although of similar blood and both being very warlike, the Maasi and Kikuyu were totally different in their living habits and appearance. The Maasi people were a pastoral society who lived almost exclusively on a gruel mixed with the milk and blood of their livestock, whereas the Kikuyu were much more agricultural, who, as almost vegetarians, maintained a diet comprised of their crops with little consumption of meat.

The Maasi warriors, called moran were extremely tall and lithe, much more so than their Kikuyu cousins and as great herders, were more mobile, always in search of new grazing land. However, both peoples were monotheists believing in a god called Ngai. As cattle represented their total wealth, they also maintained a different relationship with the roving predatory animals than the Kikuyu, such as leopard and the packs of hyena and wild dog. Their greatest enemy in that regard being the lion. Consequently, in defense of their herds, a strong hunter-prey relationship developed with the lion that supported a ritualistic presence within the Maasi tribe. The greatest honor a moran could achieve within the tribe was to singlehandedly kill a lion, an activity that maimed and killed many of the warriors. Those who survived earned great esteem and the honor of wearing a lion headdress. A less gallant achievement would be the surrounding and killing of a lion by a group of moran.

Generally, no white men were ever permitted to enter Maasi territory with the exception of Kikuyu King Boyes. And even then on a very tense basis as both the Maasi and Kikuyu were frequently at war with each other. All other whites would be immediately killed if captured while trespassing. Monti, Carrie and Kijana were momentarily unharmed by the Maasi while being escorted by the fast talking Ngomi.

Emergence of the three outsiders into the Maasi village created a mass uproar among the natives. All came storming from out of their shambas yelling and whooping. The headman confronted Ngomi who explained that the strange trio of outsiders were friends of the Kikuyu King and come in peace. And he added somberly "the two whites are witchdoctors with very strong medicine." This revelation seemed to calm the crowd.

"Come" the headman said as he motioned the intruders to follow. They entered a large shamba and were introduced to the high chief of the Maasi.

Translating through Ngomi, the chief questioned:

"Why do you enter our land?"

"Tell him we come as friends and wish to learn the ways of the Maasi" responded Monti.

"You claim to be great medicine, show us!"

Monti and Carrie both looked at each other with quizzical expressions. "What do we do now Monti?" Carrie questioned.

"I don't know, but I'll think of something" he commented as he rummaged through his medical bag.

"Aha! I'll show them some real magic!" He then drew a stethoscope from his bag. He affixed the device to his ears and as he attempted to place the chest piece on the high chief, the chief drew back in fright as the crowd of onlookers gasped and raised their weapons.

"Ngomi, tell them not to worry! This is good magic that will let the chief hear Ngai whispering to him." As this was related, the chief and his supplicants quieted. After detecting the savage's heartbeat, Monti placed the earpieces of the device to the chief's ears. The chief remained totally still as a broad smile opened across his face.

The chief immediately began mumbling in the Maasi dialect and waving about with his hands.

"What is he saying, Ngomi?"

"He talking to Ngai, Bwana. He ask for rain."

This simple stunt ennobled the white witchdoctors with the Maasi to a higher degree than anyone before. Their vaulted status rose even higher when two days later a severe thunder storm coincidently blew in convincing the tribe that their chief had a special relationship with Ngai. The downside, however, was that neither Monti nor Carrie could ever retrieve the stethoscope back from the chief. He wore the device continuously, even while sleeping. Throughout each day, he would be seen mumbling to himself conferring with Ngai as he wore the device in his ears while holding the chest piece listening to his throbbing heart.

For the next few weeks, both Monti and Carrie were held in the highest esteem by the tribe. As with the Kikuyu, the days were spent administering to the sick and wounded of the tribe and spending interminable hours with the chief and headmen discussing their habits and culture.

Their stay, however, was much more difficult than their experience with the Kikuyu, particularly in regard to their diet. The Maasi, unlike the vegetarian Kikuyu, were almost total carnivores. The staple of their diet was comprised of their peculiar porridge of blood and milk interspersed with eating raw meat. Monti and Carrie attempted to partake of this type of diet although abhorring the thought. Within a day, both became violently sick with dysentery and severe stomach cramps. For the remainder of their stay, Kijana would cook meals of mutton and various other lamb and goat dishes along with the wild vegetables he would gather.

Socially, the Maasi were different than the other tribes in the region. For example, their total dependency on their herds had ingrained the belief that Ngai had given them all of the cattle in the world. So their protection of these animals was an obsession. As such, they would never consider slaughtering any for food. Their peculiar habit was to gently open an artery in each one in turn, catching the blood and using it as an ingredient in their porridge. When completed, they would close the wound with thorn sutures. Their demeanor was also very different than that of their neighboring tribes—very proud and arrogant. Their very tall, slim build, coupled with their haughty attitude made them very imposing indeed. Monti and Carrie greatly admired their character.

Occasionally, a shauri would be held with the warriors exhibiting their unique dancing style of jumping up and down to the beat of drums.

"My Monti but they are an impressive lot in those vermillion cloaks" noted Carrie as the moran strutted and hopped during their dance.

"Yes my dear, it's not hard to understand how they rule their domain."

* * *

The days of inquiry by Monti and Carrie regarding the Maasi notion of war and the taking of life were just as fruitless as the questioning of the Kikuyu. Although appearing more intelligent than the Kikuyu, the Maasi harbored similar attitudes towards war and the killing of others. The main achievement of living with this tribe was in learning the general differences between the two war-like cultures. The two scientists decided their work was completed as they believed they had learned all they reasonably could.

thirteen

Monti and Carrie packed their meager equipment and personal belongings and had three crates of various native items shipped by caravan to the coast, they then began their cross country trek east.

They had a three day stay in Mombasa, awaiting the departure for their long sea voyage to England. On their second day in the port city, a message arrived at the hotel:

My Dear Sir:

I am troubled to have to inform you that Sherriff Watson is pursuing murder charges against Mr. Quincy Mortimer Thompson. Judge Martin is skeptical of Mr. Thompson being involved and is resisting the pursuit of any indictment. Mr. Thompson's family has hired a very prominent law firm in New York who are also arguing against the filing of charges. Both sides are now deadlocked and for now, Mr. Thompson is free.

However, both the judge and the Thompson family request your return with all haste if possible. They have great faith in your analytical skills, and considering your intimate knowledge of the ghastly past events, you above all can make sense of these issues.

Your devoted servant,
Jones

"My word Monti, this Thompson is certainly in a fix!"

"Yes dear, and if it weren't for the gravity of the charges, I would have little sympathy for him."

"Oh Monti, I think your bias against him may be slightly colored by jealously."

"Jealously? Oh, Carrie, you cut me to the quick! I simply know him to be a useless cad who preys upon unsuspecting young maidens and then breaks their heart as he moves to the next target of his desire! But we shan't leave him in the lurch, and by Jove, I do wish to catch the real devil in this. However, we still have a major commitment before us. As soon as we close this with the geographic society, we'll hasten our way back to the Park."

Their first order of business following the long journey at sea was a brief visit with Uncle Simon. He was very interested in learning of their adventures in Africa. And, during their two day visit, organized a grand dinner in their honor. They then arranged a meeting with the board of governors at the Royal Geographic Society in London as they planned to provide both a lecture and written narrative of their findings.

* * *

The geographic society president, Sir Clements Robert Markham, surprised the pair of scientists with the fanfare they received. The first night a huge banquet was held in their honor and the attendees represented many of the world's most famous explorers including the famous African adventurer and big game hunter, Frederick Courteney Selous.

"Ladies and gentlemen, thank you all for attending this evening to honor the return of two very remarkable and courageous scientists, who braved encountering and living with some of the most dangerous and primitive natives in all of Africa. We are all very anxious to learn of both their adventures and findings. So, please stand and join me in a toast for their contributions to this organization and the scientific community, but lest we not forget, also their pluck." At Markham's welcoming statement, all rose in recognition of Monti and Carrie's return clinking glasses and voicing a chorus of, "here-here!"

The next morning many hundreds of the geographic society membership including various government officials gathered in the organization's grand hall to listen to the duo's report.

Monti began the dissertation:

"Ladies and gentlemen, both Doctor Carrie Montigue-Smith and I are honored to have this great opportunity to address this assemblage. We have spent seven months in the interior of the protectorate of British East Africa, living with the tribes of both the Kikuyu and Maasi peoples. And, we must express our most sincere gratitude to the Royal Geographic Society for honoring us with its support."

Monti continued to relate in great detail their adventures and findings on the culture, living habits and endless war making of both tribes. He was frequently interrupted by loud applause and also by catcalls. In 1899, Britain was engaged in the second Boer War following the United States invading Cuba. At that time, Britain had a growing population of liberals who protested against both wars. Monti responded to the protestors by commenting, "We engaged the natives not as colonials, looking to conquer, but as scientists wishing to learn and medical doctors wishing to heal." He related their endless medical administration to the natives while weaving an interesting contrast with the native superstitions and the strong resistance they received from the native witchdoctors regarding their "white man's medicine." Following this statement, the catcalls ceased and they received a standing ovation.

As Monti provided his narration, Carrie displayed various native items pertinent to his discussion. In keeping with the Victorian conventions and attitude of the times, where women were not expected to engage in any professional careers, and particularly any dangerous pursuits, Monti did all of the talking. However, many in the audience admired Carrie and were amazed by her courage and unorthodox background.

Following their two-hour talk and commitment to provide the society with a written version of their experiences, they retired to their seats and the meeting was opened to questions from the board of governors.

"And how did you manage to pacify the natives? What type of diseases did you encounter, and how did you treat them?" etc. Both Monti and Carrie successfully fielded the questions for the next two-hours.

As the two scientists ended their talk, Sir Clements Robert Markham rose to the dais and awarded both Monti and Carrie the society's Founder's Medal. This award placed them in the pantheon of great explorers dating back sixty-seven years. They were inducted into that that august body that included such shinning lights as Captain John Hanning Speke, who in 1861 was awarded the honor "For his eminent geographical discoveries in Africa, and especially his discovery of the great lake Victoria Nyanza."

fourteen

Following a storm tossed, long voyage across the Atlantic, Monti and Carrie docked at Pier 19 in Manhattan and were met by an elated Jones.

"Oh my word Sir. It is good to see you both! And I have much news to relate." The bronzed and somewhat haggard couple embraced Jones exclaiming "Yes Jones, and we are elated to see you and be on good old American terra firma once again!"

Their arrival in Tuxedo Park created a monumental stir. The New York newspapers hailed the doctor couple, while disregarding Carrie's gender, as the new Stanley and Livingston. An afternoon banquet was held in the Tuxedo Club that necessitated the use of the entire club grounds to accommodate the enormous number of attendees. After the festivities, and numerous rounds of toasting to their honor, the exhausted couple, along with Jones retired to the manor house.

"Sir, there is much I must relate to you." Jones informed Monti in detail of the goings-on in the Park during their absence. Namely, that the judge was losing ground in keeping Quincy Mortimer Thompson out of jail.

"It's rubbish to think Thompson is guilty of murder."

"Yes Sir, I agree, but the fear within the community is so great that they will grasp upon anything. Many are convinced Mr. Thompson is the culprit and his jaded reputation doesn't help."

"That's understandable Jones, but people must consider the facts. I must speak to the judge and determine just what the legal issues are."

For a period of time, Quincy Mortimer Thompson attempted to weather the storm by nonchalantly conducting his life in the Park as usual. As the sheriff began pointing the finger of guilt in his direction, the community began to shun Thompson. Then, when horseback riding on one of the Park's bridle paths one morning, someone fired a gunshot in his direction, he considered this threat as a serious warning and booked passage on the next steamship to Europe.

J.T.

"Hello judge, it's very good to see you."

"My . . . my, Monti, it's good to see you also, and an honor it is! We've been following you and the missus' adventures in both Africa and England. We certainly have some notable residents here, but you two have placed Tuxedo Park on the international map!"

"Well, that's very kind of you judge, but I've come to speak with you on some very serious business."

"Yes, I was sure you would take this up on your return. And we were hoping that your return would not be delayed."

"Carrie and I have had a brief account of the issues from Jones. However, I'd like to hear your version of the events and also your predictions on Quincy's future in all of this."

* * *

The judge provided Monti a lengthy recounting of the two deaths as far as had been determined and offered his opinion on Thompson's legal exposure:

"Well Monti, Thompson's position in all of this is not good; you know his reputation. And this new sheriff is both a convinced and stubborn man—two difficult qualities in combination. The Park residents have been raising cane about this in both Goshen and New York City, and you know their influence."

"Yes judge, I know how blind fear can motivate people, and often in the wrong direction. But from a legal standpoint, just how exposed is Thompson?"

"Legally, evidence against him, limp as it is, is totally circumstantial. A decent defense lawyer could blow it out of court. But with juries, you never know. Until these last two deaths, the Park has managed to quash any outside reporting on the killings that you were aware of. Now however, with the new sheriff blaring this all over Goshen, the city papers picked-up on it and I'm afraid any jury selection will be biased even before setting foot in the jury box."

"Well judge, I believe we must continue to pursue the real killer, but what can Quincy do in the mean time?"

"I've heard that he's absconded to Europe. And for now, that's probably his wisest decision. Perhaps you should speak with Sherriff Watson and try to convince him that he may be on a fool's errand regarding Thompson."

Sheriff Tom Watson was a tall, slim and serious lawman. Adding to his ominous demeanor and considerable intelligence was his political connections in Goshen. He gained the office of County Sherriff via his relationship with the District Attorney, Henry Holden. The two worked on a number of high profile bank robberies when Watson was just an investigator under Holden.

"So, you are the famous Doctor James I. Montague-Smith. I've read much about you and your wife in the papers."

"Yes, I'm pleased to meet you sheriff. And I've also heard much about you" responded Monti.

"I understand that you seem to be convinced Mr. Mortimer Thompson had a hand in the deaths of Gladys Ross and Colonel McKinnon."

"Doctor, you're wrong on two counts. One- I *know* Thompson killed Ross and McKinnon, and two-, I strongly suspect he is the culprit in the other Park killings that you are familiar with."

"Sheriff, what proof do you have?"

"You know Thompson is an avid, if not famous polo player. He also is known as a despicable womanizer, liar and all around cad. On the night of Mrs. Ross's death, he had no verifiable alibi for his whereabouts, nor at the time of the colonel's death either. Of the many Park residents I've interviewed, all who know him well, claim he is capable of the murders. The boot type and size he commonly wears was in evidence at the scene of Ross's death and McKinnon was bludgeoned with a polo mallet. It's very clear he's the killer."

"I beg to disagree sheriff. And what motive would he have for killing an old school teacher that he probably didn't know and an aged war veteran?"

"Good questions my dear doctor. And what were the motives for his other unrelated killings? For example, little Tommy Baxter and the power plant operator, or the jockey?"

"I submit, those killings and these have no obvious connections. I believe they all are the acts of a very deranged mind. However, despite Thompson's well-earned reputation of being a character of ill repute, I don't believe he's a murderer. And your claim of evidence, well . . . it's very weak at best."

"Well doctor, we'll see about that in court that is, if the murderer ever returns to face his accusers."

Although both Sheriff Watson and D.A. Holden were anxious to charge and prosecute Quincy Mortimer Thompson, he had escaped their clutches. They considered dispatching a detective to locate him but first contacted Scotland Yard in London anticipating Thompson would probably take refuge with his British friends in England.
J.T.

"Carrie my love, the sheriff is a determined man, and I fear he will pin his baseless charges on poor Quincy regardless the weakness of his evidence."

"Good grief Monti, now he's 'poor Quincy'! Just recently, you were castigating him as being a despicable cad."

"His character is certainly within the bounds of serious reproach; however, he's not an evil murderer. If they proceed with charges, we must do all we can to clear his name regarding murder, not his character as a mountebank."

* * *

As Monti predicted and the sheriff surmised, Scotland Yard found Thompson living in one of London's upscale men's clubs and placed him under arrest. After being notified by the Yard, Sheriff Watson was dispatched by D.A. Holden to "sail on the next steamship available and bring the blackguard in!"

Upon his return, Thompson was incarcerated in the county jail in Goshen and charged with the murder of Colonel Henry Stafford McKinnon and Gladys Ross. Thompson's wealth enabled him to hire the law firm of Davis, Simpson and McLaren, the most prestigious and successful law firm in New York, specializing in criminal law. Benjamin Davis was one on the team defending Boss Tweed in the infamous Tammany Hall trial of the 1870s; the only case Davis, Simpson and McLaren ever lost. The day Mr. Thompson was jailed I was working at the mansion when I overheard Judge Martin asking Monti if he would work with the law firm in representing Mr. Thompson. He agreed he would.

J.T.

fifteen

"Now Monti, we must inform Benjamin Davis in great detail of everything we know about the murders and all of the parties who were, or even may have been involved in the lives of the victims, and this includes all we know of Quincy Mortimer Thompson. Both the bad and the good, the good being his nonviolent past here in the Park and any other good within him that we can discern. There will be many aggrieved husbands who would love to see him gain a seat in your newfangled electric chair. And I urge you to apply all of your analytical skills in dissecting all you can regarding the two recent deaths. I know the sheriff is stubbornly dedicated, but I don't have confidence in his skills of detection.

"I will work with Thompson's lawyers on building his defense." Replied Monti, in a stern, determined voice.

"Yes judge, I'll do all I can to exonerate Thompson, but we must also find the real killer."

Monti spent the next few days poring over the lurid past events in the Park. He and Carrie retraced their steps at all of the past crime scenes paying special attention to the murder site of Gladys Ross near the railroad siding. He spent a day in Goshen questioning Thompson in his cell and received permission, secured by the influence of Judge Martin, to inspect the polo mallet purported to be the murder weapon in the McKinnon case. The court date was set for one month henceforth and Thompson's legal team along with Judge Martin spent many days at the Goshen lockup planning his defense.

The inspection at the rail siding provided little information. It appeared that the schoolmarm was attempting to visit a student in the east end of town—the time of death being just after dark. The randomness of the crime and the fact that Ross was not robbed nor had she any enemies indicated that she was just a target of opportunity for the deranged killer. Monti learned that the condition of the body indicated the strong possibility of a struggle before she met with the speeding train. But, the sheriff neglected to offer, or even analyze any specific evidence against her death being an accident.

The polo mallet used in the colonel's murder was that of one typically used by many in that sport. Although blood stained, the sheriff claimed it contained no fingerprints, and Monti doubted if he even attempted to lift any. However, the crime was committed at the same location, the colonel's boathouse, where the Sara Mills death occurred. This indicated to Monti that the brutal death was committed by the same devil who took the life of the Mills girl.

"Carrie, it seems we are no closer to solving these crimes than we were before" commented an exasperated Monti.

"In our justice system, the accused is presumed innocent until proven guilty. I fear in this case, Thompson is guilty until we can prove he's innocent!"

"Yes dear, I tend to agree and with his reputation it won't be easy to prove his innocence."

* * *

On the opening day of the trial a large crowd had assembled in front of the old courthouse. Being the county seat and one of the first settlements in Orange County, the courthouse in Goshen dated back to before the War for Independence. Legend claimed that within the cement lintel above the entrance to the weathered brick building, the skull of the infamous Revolutionary War bandit, Claudius Smith was encased. Smith was hanged during the war as a Tory and for his depredations against the colonists.

The oak paneled courtroom was filled to capacity with those standing, reaching out to the front entrance. Besides news reporters, most came from the surrounding farm communities anxious to see a Tuxedo Park aristocrat "get his just due."

***

"Oyez, oyez" cried the Marshall of the Court. "All rise for the Honorable Judge, Malcolm Small."

Judge Malcolm Small was aptly named being only five-foot, four inches tall. His diminutive size, however, belied his fiery, no-nonsense approach to the law. While owning one of the largest dairy farms in the county, he was also a very prominent member of the local political class who maintained a severe view of crime in *his* territory.

"Please take your seats" beseeched the judge as he sat behind the bench and the twelve member jury filed in.

"The court will hear the charge of murder in the first degree for the killings of Mrs. Gladys Ross and Colonel Henry Stafford McKinnon." At that, District Attorney, Henry Holden rose to speak:

"Your Honor and ladies and gentlemen of the jury, sitting before us" as he motioned to the defendant, "Sits the most heinous killer, one who took the lives of two men, two women and one young boy."

"Objection your Honor!" Stammered Thompson's attorney, Ben Davis, as he jumped to his feet. "My client is on trial for two murders, not five."

"Objection sustained, the jury will ignore that claim. Mr. Holden, please contain yourself to the facts of the case."

"Yes your Honor. Ladies and gentlemen of the jury, the county will prove, beyond any doubt, that the defendant, Quincy Mortimer Thompson, in callous cold blood, took the lives of the aged, Mrs. Gladys Ross, a poor defenseless school teacher and Colonel Henry Stafford McKinnon, a noble member of our community who served with honor and bravery in defense of the Union in the War Between the States. These despicable acts were perpetrated by a son of wealth and privilege. Unlike his two helpless victims, members of our community who had unflinchingly served us all for many years, Mr. Thompson did not ever serve his nation or the community. But rather spent his days

gallivanting and carousing with the moneyed class of
Tuxedo Park. In fact, when he knew that the wheels of
justice were on his heels, he absconded to London, living in
luxury to avoid answering to his crimes."

Throughout this dissertation, the public became more
and more restless, with many of the men murmuring
obscenities at Thompson under their breath as some
women began to weep causing Small to rap his gavel.

Next, Ben Davis rose to address the jury:

"Ladies and gentlemen, you all are residents of this fine
old community of Goshen, New York. I don't need to remind
you of the patriotic and gallant past of this town. During the
War for Independence, your forefathers stood for truth and
freedom, thereby resisting the tyranny of the crown. You
exercised truth and justice in capturing, trying and
punishing that scoundrel, Claudius Smith; a just and noble
effort. You have, time and again, displayed your love and
faith in the virtue of justice. Therefore, you will recognize the
folly of Mr. Holden's charges and the innocence of my client,
Mr. Quincy Mortimer Thompson. I will absolutely prove,
that is, prove not on the basis of rumor, or shallow and
meager circumstantial evidence, but on proof that Mr.
Thompson is innocent of these erroneous charges. And I
know and trust that in your sense of fair play and common
sense you will arrive at the obvious decision of not guilty."

At the end of the opening statements, Judge Small
retired the court for the day.

"Well judge, what do you think of today's proceedings?"
Questioned Monti.

"Monti my friend, Judge Small is a tough old buzzard,
but he is fair. However, I'm concerned with the jury. They
all come from the soil, farmers, share croppers and so
forth. They may not look upon a wealthy Park resident
fairly. But I must say, the defense attorney put on a good
show for the first day."

Day two was the prosecutor's calling of witnesses as he
built his case.

His first calling was the old constable. The retired cop
limped up to the witness box with a weed stem dangling
from his mouth. As he approached the bench, Judge Small

glared at him and stated in a loud voice, "Constable, the court would be very pleased for you to remove that foreign object from your yap!" At this the crowd broke into laughter and catcalls. "That will be enough before I clear the courtroom!" The judge admonished.

"So Constable" the prosecutor asked, "Tell the court your relationship with Tuxedo Park and your knowledge of the defendant."

"Well, I'm now retired, but I was the Town of Tuxedo Constable for thirty-years. I've know Mr. Quincy Mortimer Thompson for most of this time. We weren't bosom buddies though, I only knew him from an official standpoint."

"Tell us about his character."

"Objection. Your honor the witness states he only knew the defendant officially. So he's not in a position to judge character."

Carrie whispered, "My word Monti, he wants a character to judge a character."

"Objection sustained."

"Constable, do you know if the defendant personally knew the deceased, Sara Mills?"

"Yes, he personally knew her."

"Objection your Honor. The death of Miss Mills has not been shown to have any bearing on this case. The prosecutor is simply on a fishing expedition."

"Mr. Holden, can you show a direct link between the Ross and McKinnon killings with the Mills death?"

"Well, err . . . not at this time your Honor."

"Then objection sustained."

"Then I have no further questions for the constable your Honor."

"Mr. Davis, do you wish to question the constable?"

"No questions at this time your Honor."

* * *

The next witness called was Sheriff Tom Watson.

"Sheriff, did you investigate the murders of Mrs. Gladys Ross and Colonel Henry Stafford McKinnon?"

"Yes sir. I did."

"Tell us first the details of the Ross murder. Where and when did you find her?"

"I was in my Tuxedo Town office about 8:30 P.M when a young boy came in saying a body was found near the train station. I then proceeded to the station and found the body of Gladys Ross about six feet from the tracks just north of the station."

"What was her condition?"

"Very mangled."

"Was there any sign of a struggle?"

"Yes, I think so."

"What did you do next?"

"I investigated the area and immediately found boot prints."

"Tell us about the boot prints."

"Well, they clearly were that of a man; riding boots of a fairly large size."

"Did you find anything else?"

"No."

"I then called the coroner to remove the body."

"How did you proceed with the investigation?"

"I was told by the town judge, which is Judge Martin, that a Doctor Montague-Smith found boot tracks that were associated with the Sara Mills murder and made a plaster cast of them. I then learned that the doctor's servant, a Mr. Jones had access to them. Mr. Jones then showed them to me and I'm sure that they were from the same boots."

"And then what did you do?"

"After interviewing a number of the town and Park folk, I learned that Mr. Quincy Mortimer Thompson was a famous polo player and frequently wore riding boots. When I went to see him, I learned two things, he had no verifiable alibi for the night of the murder and in fact, when I met him and questioned him in the jail, he was wearing a pair of large size riding boots."

"Tell us about your investigation of the colonel's murder."

"I was once again summoned to respond to a murder scene, this time in Tuxedo Park. It was at the mansion of Colonel Henry Stafford McKinnon where I found his crumpled body. He was lying in his boathouse, his head bashed-in with a polo mallet lying by his side. In fact, he was lying at precisely the same spot as the Mills girl was claimed to be found.

"I then immediately interrogated Mr. Thompson. He claimed to know nothing about the death, but, he once again could not account for his movement for the entire period."

"Then what did you do?"

"I advised Mr. Thompson to remain in the area, and as you know, I came to consult with you."

"Yes and how were you advised?"

"Well, you directed me to immediately place Mr. Thompson into custody. When I returned to Tuxedo Park, Mr. Thompson's butler informed me that he hurriedly packed some bags and left. Following this, I learned he rushed to the train station for New York where he boarded a boat for England."

At this statement, the previously hushed crowd in the courtroom released an audible sound of shock and anger.

Carrie mumbled to herself, "Now he's sunk!"

"So sheriff, now what did you do?"

"Objection your Honor, he's been leading the witness!"

"Objection overruled."

"As you directed me, I booked passage on the next steamship after wiring Scotland Yard. When I arrived in London I placed Mr. Thompson under arrest."

"I have no further questions your Honor."

* * *

At this juncture, defense attorney, Benjamin Davis rose to question the witness.

"Sheriff Watson, beginning with the death of Mrs. Ross, why did you conclude she was the victim of a struggle, and not just the subject of a tragic accident?"

"Well, besides the boot prints, there were signs in the dirt of a scuffle."

As he paced the floor looking down, the canny defense attorney wheeled around and peppered the sheriff:

"Speaking of boot prints sheriff, why didn't you take plaster casts like the doctor had at the Mills murder scene?"

"I guess it just didn't occur to me."

"Would you say that would have been proper police procedure?"

"Well . . . er . . . I guess so."

"So would you consider the absence of taking plaster casts sloppy police work?"

"Objection your Honor! He's badgering the witness."

"Objection sustained."

"I withdraw the question. Again, regarding the boot prints, why do you think they were made by the defendant?"

"They were of a large size . . . "

"But you don't know the exact size because you neglected to take a casting?"

"Well yes, but I know big feet when I see them!"

This inane response drew loud laughter from the crowd.

"Order in the court" demanded the judge.

Davis continued:

"What size do you guess the prints were?"

"I would say they were size eleven, or perhaps larger."

"What size boot does the defendant wear?"

"Size eleven."

Mr. Davis addressed the judge:

"Your Honor, I wish to present into evidence, this survey conducted by the esteemed Judge Martin. He questioned all of the polo-playing members of the Tuxedo Club regarding their foot sizes. Of the twenty-two members, six are a size eleven and two are a size eleven and a half, and one is a gargantuan size twelve. This does not include the numerous riding public in Orange County nor the transient polo players who frequent the Park on occasion.

"Sheriff, have you questioned all of the big footed polo players living in the Park and all horseback riders in Orange County with big feet as to their whereabouts on the night of the Ross murder?"

The flush faced sheriff commented:

"No."

Following this line of questioning, the crowd roared with delight as Judge Small frantically slammed his gavel down. When order was restored, the defense attorney continued his questioning:

"So sheriff, regarding the polo mallet found at the scene of the colonel's murder. Did you take finger prints from the murder weapon?"

The clearly intimidated sheriff responded, "No."

"Did it slip your mind like you neglected to take castings at the Ross murder scene?"

"Objection, the counselor is once again badgering."

Objection sustained. Mr. Davis, I must warn you to cease needling the witness."

"Yes your Honor, I withdraw the question."

"Do you think anyone else in the Park may own a polo mallet sheriff?"

"Quite possibly, I guess."

"And how many do you think exist?"

After a long hesitation, the judge interjected, "Please answer the question sheriff."

"Well, I don't rightly know."

In a condescending manner, Davis stated, "Sheriff, I can help, many dozens of polo mallets exist in the Park."

As many members of the jury had farms to tend to during this time of season, the court sessions were held to a minimum each day. At the end of this line of questioning, Judge Small recessed for the day.

That evening, Benjamin Davis and Judge Martin had dinner with Monti and Carrie at the Tuxedo Club.

"Doctor Montague-Smith," "Please call me Monti, counselor." "Monti, I'd like to place you on the stand. With the gravity of your professional reputation and your astute knowledge of the Park murders, I think you could be a big asset for the defense."

"But I thought the other murders were off limits for the trial?"

"No, not anymore. I'm sure I can now introduce the previous killings into evidence. And besides, during some of those events Thompson may be able to present valid alibis for his whereabouts. If you can link all the murders to one killer, then we can prove his innocence."

The judge interjected, "I agree with Davis, Monti. Additionally, the jury will respect anything you have to say regarding the murders and Quincy's character."

"Monti, I also agree, you can't sit on the sidelines if you can assist in the acquittal of an innocent man, even if you don't personally like him" commented Carrie."

* * *

"I wish to call to the stand an expert witness who besides being an internationally known expert in the science of murder analysis; he is also very familiar with the other murders that have occurred in Tuxedo Park. And since the questioning of Sheriff Watson opened this path during his testimony, the experiences of Doctor Montague-Smith will be very relevant. So your Honor, I call Doctor James I. Montague-Smith to the stand."

D. A. Holden immediately jumped up declaring, "Objection your Honor, Constable Dillon's testimony regarding the other Park murders was denied under Mr. Davis' objection, now he wants to probe the same topics with his witness!"

Waving his finger at the prosecutor, Judge Small responded, "No, no, no Mr. Holden, as the councilor stated, you opened this line of questioning with Sheriff Watson's testimony. Don't worry, you'll have your crack at this witness."

The courtroom crowd applauded as Monti walked to the bench and was sworn in while the reporters ran for their telephones.

The defense council began their questioning:

"Doctor Montague-Smith, as being called as an expert witness, could you please provide the court with a brief curriculum vitae?"

"Certainly sir. My education is in both the medical and engineering fields. I have a Doctorate in Medicine from Columbia College and a Masters Degree in Mechanical Engineering from King's College, London. I have conducted research in the criminal mind at Sing Sing Penitentiary, I've spent nine months studying the warlike tribes of Central Africa, and for an extended period I have lived with the Zulu Nation. I'm a Fellow of the Royal Geographic Society in London where I've recently been awarded the

Founder's Medal. As a sideline activity, I've been studying the effects of gravity on human organs, the electrical impulses that may trigger thought in the brain and the lifecycle and mating habits of the fruit fly." This last description of Monti's interests elicited smirks and hushed laughter from the audience warranting another slam of the judge's mallet.

"So now doctor," as the defense council began, "Have you studied the details surrounding the deaths of Gladys Ross and Colonel McKinnon?"

"Yes sir, I have."

"And do you believe these murders are related in any way to the earlier killings in the Park?"

"Yes sir, I do."

"Please tell the court why."

"To begin with, the Town of Tuxedo, including the Park, in fact counting in the entire county, has never witnessed such an explosion of vicious murders in such a short period of time, even counting the bloody killings during the Eastern Indian Wars; Chief Joseph Brant's depredations and so forth. The other fact is that the frequency of the random killings fit a pattern that we have been noticing in recent years. An example being the Jack the Ripper murders in Whitechapel, London during the 1880s.

"This pattern is representative of a very deranged but exceedingly clever mind that takes great pleasure in the fear and suffering of others. An individual who gains excitement and self-esteem in the challenge of outsmarting and eluding law enforcement. Notwithstanding the mysterious ending of the Ripper murders, this type of individual will continue with his evil doings until captured or he meets his own death."

"So you think the recent killings fit this pattern of derangement and were committed by the same person?"

"Absolutely sir."

"Are you acquainted with the defendant, Mr. Thompson?"

"Yes, I know him well, spanning a number of years."

"From your research into the criminal mind, do you believe he committed any of these murders?"

"Certainly not."

"And why not?"

"His character is that of a lazy, benign person, totally committed to a life of ease, pleasure and self-indulgence. Furthermore, I don't think he has the cunning to have executed these murders in such a clever manner. That's not to say that a deranged killer couldn't present a very misleading front, but from my researching criminals over the years, and my familiarity with Mr. Thompson, well, I just don't believe this level of viciousness is in him."

"Once again, so you think the multitude of killings were performed by the same person and you don't think Mr. Thompson is the culprit?"

"I'm ninety-nine percent sure."

"Thank you doctor. No further questions your Honor."

As Monti contemplated his last statement, he felt unease in leaving out the one percent possibility of Thompson's being guilty, but as a scientist, and without the absolute certainty of exonerating proof, he couldn't be totally sure. The prosecutor immediately zeroed in on this:

"Doctor Smith, in your first statement, you claimed 'certainly not' when asked if Mr. Thompson committed the crimes, yet you then left a degree of uncertainty in your following statement, that is a one percent possibility. I mean to say you left the door open, so which is it?" Then in a loud voice, Holden questioned, "Could he have committed the murders?"

"Well, er, yes, without dead certain proof, anyone could have committed the murders."

"That's not what I asked, doctor. Could the defendant have committed the murders?"

"Objection your Honor, the witness already answered the question."

"Objection sustained."

Over dinner that night, following the dramatic day in court, Carrie became critical of what she believed was Monti's vacillating, seemingly inconsistent testimony.

"Monti, you have left a degree of doubt regarding Thompson's innocence, this may sink him with the jury!"

"Carrie, I just couldn't speak in absolutes. As scientists, we deal with probability and in Thompson's case, the personality indicators point very strongly that he is not our man. But it would be disingenuous if I placed a one-hundred percent probability on his innocence."

"Oh Monti, sometimes you must offer the benefit of the doubt."

"That my dear, is the job of the jury."

* * *

The final witness to be called by the defense, was Quincy Mortimer Thompson. Although his attorney knew having a defendant on the witness stand was a chancy maneuver, subjecting him to cross examination by the prosecutor. But Davis felt his client had solid proof of his innocence. And the most dramatic way to release this to the jury was by his own words.

"I wish to call as my last witness your Honor, Quincy Mortimer Thompson." As Davis announced this, even the members of the jury gasped as all in attendance leaned forward in their seats. Thompson approached the witness stand decked-out in an elegant three-piece suit, and *not* wearing any riding boots.

Defense attorney Davis had the first questioning session:

"Mr. Thompson, please inform the court of your whereabouts and the schedule of your movements on the night of the murder of Sara Mills."

"Well sir. I was in attendance at the Tuxedo Park Autumn Ball. I arrived at the club at around 7:30 and remained there until the search party began scouring the Park for Sara. Err, I mean Miss Mills. We left the club and went on the search at around 11 and I continued with the search party until sunup."

"Does that mean you were in the company of others the whole time?"

"Yes, I was."

"The day of the horse race, when the jockey was shot from his horse, or rather when the horse was shot from under the jockey, where were you when this occurred?"

"I was sitting in the reserved section of the stands with the other notables from the Park."

"Very well Mr. Thompson, I needn't question your whereabouts during all of the other murders. You clearly couldn't have committed all of these crimes if you have witnesses for your presence during the first two crimes, could you?"

The prosecutor cut in, "I have objections your Honor on a number of issues in this line of questioning. First, are we to take Mr. Thompson's word regarding these witnesses? Who are they? Secondly, this presupposes a single murderer. Are we convinced all of the killings were committed by the same murderer; I'm not, and last, we need to know his whereabouts during the Gladys Ross and Colonel McKinnon's murders?"

As Judge Small sustained the objection, he winced at the thought of calling a long string of additional witnesses that would delay an already long, drawn-out trial, adding:

"Don't worry Mr. Holden, I'm sure we'll hear from additional witnesses and we'll learn just where the defendant was or was not during all of the murders." The judge finished his sentence as he glared at the defendant.

Holden responded, "I wish to defer additional questioning of this witness to a later time your Honor."

"Mister Davis, do you wish to question Mr. Thompson?"

"I also wish to defer questioning and I would like to request a three day recess to enable us to accommodate the prosecutor's suggestion of calling additional witnesses for the defense your Honor."

With tongue in cheek the judge responded:

"Gentlemen it's so refreshing to see the prosecutor supporting the testimony of defense witnesses, also quite unorthodox. But I will grant the recess. This session is ended." And at that, he rapped his gavel.

The next few days were a frantic process of interviewing the potential witnesses to support Thompson's alibi for the time of the various Park murders. The canvassing of the many people were divided between Monti, Carrie and Judge Martin. Some didn't remember seeing Thompson at the many venues he claimed, others simply either didn't wish to be involved and some simply disliked the accused and were happy to see him get convicted. However, there were enough who remembered his whereabouts and were willing to testify for his defense. But, there were no witnesses for his activities on the nights Ross and the colonel were murdered.

When court was reconvened, the eleven defense witnesses were grilled by both Holden and Davis. And Thompson was recalled to the stand for questioning, first by D. A. Holden.

"Mr. Thompson, you seem to be covered for your whereabouts during the first Park murders. Now please inform the court of where you were during the night of Mrs. Ross's death."

"I ah, spent the night with a friend."

"Who?"

"Well ah, I'm not in a position to state who."

"So you claim to be with a friend the night of Mrs. Ross's murder but you're not in a position to state who it was? Could it be you were not with anyone, but rather were out stalking and killing poor Mrs. Ross?" The prosecutor shouted in accusation.

"Objection your Honor. The prosecutor is deciding the answer to his own question."

"Objection sustained. Mr. Thompson, I suggest you answer the questions fully."

"Your Honor, it would be impolite for me to disclose who I was with that night."

The prosecutor once again quizzed Thompson as to who he was with. And once again, he refused to answer.

"All right, so you claim you were with this phantom person the night of the Ross murder, who you won't name. Where were you on the night Colonel Henry Stafford McKinnon was bludgeoned to death?"

"I was at home."

"Who can verify that?"

"I was alone all night."

"Ah, so in reality, you can't verify your whereabouts or actions on either night of the two murders. I have no further questions your Honor."

It was now the defense attorney's opportunity to try and smooth over the damage resulting from Thompson's stubbornness in refusing to name the mysterious person he spent the night with during the Ross murder. Davis spent hours with Thompson in his cell the night before attempting to impress upon him the importance of coming clean. "Are you aware that your life hangs in the balance? Even if you divulge the person's name, thereby establishing an alibi, we still have an uphill fight!"

* * *

"Mr. Thompson, so far you are cleared in any of the Park murders . . . except for the nights of the Ross and McKinnon deaths. I know you, being a gentleman, are reluctant to possibly blemish anyone's reputation, but you must state where you were and whom you were with on the night of Ross's murder."

Reluctantly, Thompson stated: "Mr. Davis, I spent the night in a Middletown hotel with Mrs. Haggerty."

At the disclosure the Tuxedo Park mayor's wife was sleeping with Thompson sent the court spectators into a near riot forcing Judge Small to threaten clearing the courtroom.

"And where were you on the night of the colonel's death?"

"As I have stated over and over, I was home alone all night! I was nursing a bad hangover from the night before at the club and went to bed early, alone."

Jean Haggerty was later called to the stand to verify Thompson's claim. She tearfully admitted to having an affair with Thompson and spending the night with him while her husband was in Manhattan attending a political meeting.

The courtroom revelation of Thompson and the mayor's wife, Jean Haggerty, created an uproar in the Park. Tom Haggerty was forced to resign his position as mayor and both he and Jean placed their house on the market and immediately left the Park; never to be heard from again.
J.T.

sixteen

Much to the relief of Judge Small, the trial was finally nearing its end with the prosecutor providing his closing argument:

"Ladies and gentlemen of the jury, you have dutifully sat through numerous hours of testimony regarding the violent deaths of six of our dear neighbors. However, the defense team, including its so called expert doctor, wishes you to believe they were all murdered by the same person. And why would the defense team try to convince you of this? Simply because the defendant has alibis for some of these murders, but not all.

"The murders were committed at different times, at different places and all in a different manner, but yet, the defense claims they all occurred under the hand of one person. I submit to you the real issue in this trial are the deaths of Mrs. Ross and Colonel Henry Stafford McKinnon! So we have learned Mr. Thompson had an alibi due to his purported immoral and underhanded liaison with Mrs. Haggerty, a relationship that destroyed a family and embarrassed Tuxedo Park. His alibi may or may not be valid. We all know how feelings of the heart can distort someone's honesty, so I'll leave the validity of this alibi to you all to ponder. And then we have the excuse of Mr. Thompson sleeping through the murder of the colonel, a slumber that he cannot substantiate. A very unlikely excuse!

"The wisdom and honor of your final decision not only impinges upon the memory of, and justice due to the victims, but to the justice due to the entire county. So therefore, I call upon your good sense and convict this heinous killer of the two murders of poor Gladys Ross and the gallant Colonel McKinnon. I rest my case."

This speech drew a standing ovation from the spectators, even some members of the jury applauded. The power of his dissertation also elicited a disheartened feeling of loss in Monti.

"Oh my dear, even William Jennings Bryan couldn't top such an emotional closing. I fear we are sunk in the eyes of the jury."

***

The attorney for the defense, Benjamin Davis then rose to speak. He paced back and forth in front of the jury box with his head down as he began his closing:

"Ladies and gentlemen, what you have just heard was a clever effort by the prosecutor to both distort the facts of this case and focus your attention not on the gravity of the evidence, but on a few issues which Mr. Holden desperately believes is the only way he can prevail. And his effort to convict an innocent man, if successful, will not only be a horrible miscarriage of justice, but will leave this community still in the clutches of a violent murderer.

"The relationship of *all* of these crimes to one another, not just two, but all of them very clearly points to the evil doings of one, not two, or three, or four, but one despicable killer. Are we to believe we have a gang of killers roaming about; taking these lives for no reason? The type of deranged mind that the immanent Doctor Montigue-Smith described is rare, very rare. But I'm sad to say, occasionally happens. So, to believe that a dark cloud of multiple lunatics that have simultaneously descended upon this community is ridiculous.

"So if you exercise the common sense that I know you all have ladies and gentlemen, you simply cannot buy Mr. Holden's nonsensical theory. Therefore, we are clearly dealing with one individual who perpetrated all of this evil over many nights. Nights that as the many witnesses have stated, under oath, nights that the defendant was not out stalking, but was with them.

"Regarding the tragic deaths of Mrs. Ross and the colonel, we heard the tearful admission of Mrs. Haggerty.

Yet, Mr. Holden was very willing to impugn her integrity. Can we really believe Mrs. Haggerty is a liar? A liar willing to destroy her family simply to lie about a one night tryst? I don't believe so.

"And the colonel. The defendant said he slept through the night, never leaving his home. Haven't some of you spent the night on occasion alone, nursing a throbbing head? I have! And many know Mr. Thompson to be a bachelor, man-about-town who likes to party and imbibe on occasion.

"The judge will instruct you, I'm sure, on the principal of 'reasonable doubt.' And just what does that mean? According to the law dictionary, 'Beyond a Reasonable Doubt: is the standard that must be met by the prosecution's evidence in a criminal prosecution: that no other logical explanation can be derived from the facts except that the defendant committed the crime, thereby overcoming the presumption that a person is innocent until proven guilty. So let's analyze how this applies in this case:

"First, regardless of the aspersions Mr. Holden accuses Mrs. Haggerty of committing, is her testimony beyond a reasonable doubt? No. The claim that Mr. Thompson fell asleep the night of the colonel's murder, is that beyond reasonable doubt? Has any evidence been raised that the defendant is an intransigent liar? No. So considering these facts, you must find Mr. Thompson, not guilty. I rest my case your Honor."

Judge Small instructed the jury on the fine points to consider in the case and reiterated Mr. Davis's definition of reasonable doubt. However, he completed his charge to the jury with one caveat:

"Ladies and gentlemen, I have the disappointing obligation to sequester you all until your deliberations are complete and you render a verdict. The amount of publicity this case has generated just presents the possibility that some bias or misinformation could creep into your thoughts. I know Independence Day is this weekend, and the sequestration may deny you the opportunity for celebrations, but you reaching a verdict is too important to sacrifice for any festivities. And naturally, I do not expect you to rush your deliberations to attend a fireworks demonstration or a picnic."

* * *

"So Judge" questioned Monti, "How do you think the jury will vote?"

"Frankly, I am very apprehensive for Thompson's future. Although both you and Davis offered logical answers to the prosecutor's claims, Holden presented a very strong closing argument. I just don't know."

"Yes, I fear the combination of Thompson's poor reputation as a philandering gadfly coupled with his being a wealthy 'Parkie' will bias the jury against him."

"Oh Monti dear, you are too cynical. I completely trust in the good sense and fair play of the common man" Carrie chimed in. "And besides, we will be having a wonderful time on the fourth, so look on the bright side!"

Everyone in the Park and not least of all the participants in the trial were relieved when it all ended. However, speculation on how the jury would decide caused quite a stir. In fact, the local gamblers were placing ten to one odds that Thompson would be found guilty and much money began changing hands.

Regarding the July 4th celebrations, the Park planned to hold their traditional fireworks display and picnic. The Park elders even condescendingly acquiesced each year to open the front gates to the Park permitting the town 'riff-raff' entry to participate in this well anticipated event.

J.T.

The annual Tuxedo Park Independence Day Event always created a great stir in the normally staid enclave. Days before the celebration, Park attendants trimmed trees, hung banners and tidied-up in every nook and cranny of the two-thousand acre community. The Park fathers even had arranged for a horse-drawn, steam calliope to travel the Park's roads spreading musical merriment. The day routinely would draw close to three-thousand attendees.

The warm, sunny morning of the fourth, began with speeches by local politicians and the playing of patriotic music by a number of local high school bands. The afternoon schedule included a horserace competition by the Park's equestrian community with the grand finale being an enormous fireworks display over Tuxedo Lake after sundown.

As the evening wore on, crowds began to cluster on the green expanse of lawn bordering the west side of the lake. Numerous blankets and beach chairs were occupied by the many families living in the region as they began to settle down in anticipation of the pyrotechnic event. Monti, Carrie, and the judge settled into the comforts of the veranda at the Jacob Mills estate, just mere yards from the lake where Sara disappeared two years before.

"This is a wonderful vantage point Monti, and we couldn't have asked for a more pleasant evening weather wise."

"Yes my dear" commented Monti as he sipped his glass of chardonnay and puffed on his pipe.

As the small group was relaxing in the warm breeze of dusk, Jones entered with a message for Monti from Ben Davis.

"Doctor, the jury just rendered a verdict of guilty of murder in the first degree. This will automatically trigger an appeal. Our next step must be a detailed analysis of the case, where we may have gone wrong the first time, and plan a new approach. Sorry to inform you of the bad news on Independence Day. Davis"

"Good heavens, it's just as I thought, we've lost, and they've convicted Quincy of murder in the first degree!" Exclaimed Monti.

* * *

Just as Monti finished reading the message to the group, the first aerial blast of a multi-colored, starlight charge lit the night sky over the lake. The rockets went aloft at two to three minute intervals with their booming reverberating across the hills surrounding the lake.

"My god Monti what bad news to receive on such a festive occasion" commented the judge.

"Well judge, I'm glad someone is finally being brought to justice for the killing of my daughter. I never did trust that Thompson scoundrel. And the lurid way he used to gawk at poor Sara!" commented Mrs. Mills.

"I understand your anger Agnes, but in our pursuit of justice, we must ensure the right culprit is punished. We mustn't indict someone who may be the wrong man!"

The group sat quietly watching the bang and boom of the many fireworks; a star shell, then a spray of multicolored sparks, then a large fountain of white streaks. Finally the grand finale produced an array of numerous small bomblets that erupted just as the band across the lake reached the 'finis coronat opus' of the 1812 Overture.

Before the immense crowd on the green even began to rise from their seats, a huge roar accompanied by a tremendous lighting of the sky to the east shook all in attendance. The blast reverberated back and forth across the lake while the sky brightened over the forest in the direction of the powerhouse.

"My god Monti, what was that?" shouted the judge.

"It's near the powerhouse, I'm going there" exclaimed Monti as he ran to the front of the mansion. Two horses were tethered to the hitching post near the mansion's porte-cochere. He jumped upon the best appearing mount and galloped to the Ramapo River as fast as the steed would carry him.

The powerhouse was located about two miles from the Park gate and was situated on the bank of the river to draw its cooling water. Monti surmised the huge fireball must have been caused by the large fuel oil storage tank burning, but what accounted for the massive blast was preying on his mind as he rode.

He was greeted by the sight of only brick rubble remaining of the former powerhouse with the charred remains of the turbine generator projecting above. The steam engine's boiler was burst open as a huge wall of fire danced upon the crumpled remains of the fuel oil tank. The air was filled with burning oil fumes. The heat was so intense, he had to tether the horse a considerable distance away from the burning mass.

Monti's first impulse was to find the plant operator. The control shack was a short distance on the opposite side of the powerhouse, somewhat protected from the blast effect and burning tank. Although filled with smoke and blown out windows, the shack was otherwise untouched by the blast. As he opened the door, Monti was shocked to find the plant operator slumped over his desk. He was face down with the back of his head parted by a huge gash. Lying on the desk next to him was a large bloody crowbar.

Monti instantly rushed out the door as his eyes fell upon the form of a large man emerging from the smoke. He walked with a limp, face and head covered by a balaclava and he was clearly armed.

"So, we meet again doctor" he growled in a quiet voice. "I told you I would continue to play with you and your arrogant, elitist Park neighbors. And the funniest thing is that the most arrogant of all the elitists is being blamed for my handiwork!"

"How did you do all of this?"

"Not hard. First I sent your man to endless sleep in the shack, then I raised the boiler pressure and locked the relief valve, and then I deposited fifty pounds of dynamite around the tank and watched the fun begin. I actually out did your measly fireworks and provided a much more dramatic July 4, celebration. Did you enjoy it?"

"Your cleverness has backfired, now it will be known that the mad killer is still running loose, and it's not Thompson."

"Not necessarily, when I kill you, I'll place the bodies in such a position to indicate you killed the operator after learning he blew the site. I'll place the gun in his hand; he simply mortally wounded you as you clubbed him to death. All I have to do is shoot you so you bleed-out slowly and Thompson will still be on the hot seat."

To carry out his evil plan, the killer needed to shoot Monti from a very close distance to ensure the deposit of the telltale powder deposits and stippling of a close shot, furthermore, he wanted to aim the gun in such a manner to sever Monti's femoral artery which would cause a massive bleeding to take killing effect within minutes. In theory, this would provide just enough time for Monti to have bludgeoned the operator. His additional challenge was to accomplish this inside the operator's shack so as to not leave a blood trail outdoors. All of these considerations provided a very difficult set of moves.

"All right doctor, turn around and enter the shack." Monti's quick mind realized the killer's goal and he slowly walked back into the shack. "Now turn around." As he was swinging around, Monti deflected the killer's gun hand. The force of the block discharged the pistol and the stray round hit Monti in his upper thigh. But as he knocked the gun hand with his left, he landed a hard right to the killer's chin knocking him to the floor. The killer immediately sprang to his feet and headed into the night as Monti grasped the pistol from the floor and stumbled after him. The killer jumped upon a horse he had tethered in the woods and rode off.

Despite bleeding significantly, Monti struggled into the saddle and galloped up the road to the Orange Turnpike. At the top of the hill he saw the killer turn and ride toward the village of Sloatsburg. Struggling to remain in the saddle, Monti thought he heard the galloping of horses behind him. Carrie, Jones and the judge spied the two as they passed the Park's gate and began to race down the dirt road in pursuit. The killer continued thundering down the turnpike to the next village with the impromptu posse close behind. When reaching the village, he dove off of his horse and burst through the doors of a local roadhouse grabbing a woman who was just about to leave.

Monti nearly fell from his horse and stumbled into the building to find the woman with a knife at her throat while in the arms of the killer.

"Stand back or I'll slit her throat!" Warned the killer. Just then two of the three following riders entered. "Stand back I said!"

"Drop the knife, you can't escape" ordered the judge as the terrified woman began whimpering.

The group, along with the killer stood stock still in a standoff. "Listen" said Monti, "Release the woman, there is no way you can escape." Just then a shot rang out as the killer slumped to the floor with a bullet through his head. Jones, having entered through a back door, stood at the end of the room with his smoking pistol still in the aiming position. Monti blurted out, "Jones, by Jove, just in time!" The judge walked over to the corpse and deftly removed the balaclava as Carrie gasped, "Oh my word, it's the old constable!"

**

Very few if any in Tuxedo could imagine how the lame, ex-constable, Charlie Dillon, who, in retirement had degenerated into becoming the town drunk, was actually the evil but brilliant scourge who was terrorizing the community for the last few years. Even Monti had difficulty reconciling the extremes in his character. Carrie wondered how the constable managed to baffle perhaps the world's most astute researcher in the science of deranged crime for so long. Following the startling revelation of who was terrifying the community, Quincy Thompson was immediately released from jail.

During Monti's recovery from the leg wound, he and Carrie held a small celebratory party with Carrie's father, the town judge and Benjamin Davis in attendance; with Jones being feted as the special guest of honor. Part way through the festivities, Sheriff Tom Watson appeared at the manor house requesting to urgently speak to Monti in private.

**

"Doctor Montague-Smith, I have some startlingly dreadful news to inform you, another gruesome murder has been committed!"

After recalling these gruesome events in Tuxedo Park, so many years ago, I will close by relating only a few but not all of the events that followed. The enormous power exerted by the influential titans of the Park ensured the print media would drop any further investigating or reporting. Once the court case against Mr. Thompson ended, the dark days preceding those events faded from public memory as cigar smoke drifts away and disintegrates on the wind; but only for a period of time.

When learning that the evil terror being inflected upon the community over such a protracted period of time was initiated by the bumbling alcoholic constable, the town folk and Park residents were simply disbelieving. Their apprehensions were well founded with the events that later surfaced; a heinous plot, so dastardly in its potential, which I cannot even divulge here.

Monti and Carrie were totally vexed with the discovery of Constable Charlie Dillon being the perpetrator of so many dastardly crimes. This revelation initiated both an in-depth study of Dillon's background by the pair and a new round of debate as to underlying cause.

Although a well-respected western lawman in his earlier days, Monti and Carrie traced his early upbringing to the Town of Tuxedo, when that community was just being formed as a shanty town for the new immigrants imported to build Lorillard's new utopia behind the gate. They worked as laborers toiling on the miles of roads and stone walls encircling the new Park. Living in squalor as the New York swells were building their mansions imbued Dillon with a deep sense of hatred for the wealthy. His early experiences as a lawman, continuously engaged in the pursuit of western bad men, developed skills enabling him to evade detection. However, while pouring over old records and news articles in the New York City police archives, the pair of sleuths also learned Dillion was discharged from the Pinkerton's for excessive brutality with prisoners he would capture and bring in. These new revelations continued the ongoing debate between Monti and Carrie; is the evil mind created by life experiences, or an innate derangement or both?

* * *

Quincy Mortimer Thompson, similar to the Haggertys was ostracized by the community and eventually moved from the Park and disappeared from sight. Doctors James I. Montague-Smith and Carrie Montague-Smith were tragically lost on the night of 15 April, 1912 when the Titanic went down in the north Atlantic. They were returning from another Royal Geographic Society sponsored expedition to Africa. The gallant Jones, devastated by the loss of his employers, retired to England. The venerable Judge Martin lived a long and fruitful life serving in the Wilson administration at the Treaty of Versailles following the Great War.

Here I am in my twilight years working at the manor house as the grounds keeper for James I. Montague-Smith, Junior.

So in closing, I stand as your servant, with my deepest sincerity,
John Thomas
December 25, 1951